There was something about her.

Maybe it was the way she carried herself, shoulders back and chin lifted.

Noticing him for the first time, she grabbed his hand in hers. "Pastor Mason, how nice of you to come."

Wade tried to ignore the jolt of electricity that shot up his arm and sent his heart pounding. He looked into her eyes and prayed she couldn't see the attraction he felt. "Call me Wade."

He noted a glimmer of interest in her eyes before she looked away. "I've never called a pastor by his first name."

"You've probably never had a pastor your age."

Kristy gazed back at him, and he felt her scrutiny from his head to his toes. Finally, she smiled, exposing a dimple in her left cheek he hadn't noticed before.

Jennifer Collins Johnson and her husband have been married for over two decades. They have three daughters and one son-in-law. Jennifer is a sixth-grade language arts teacher. She is also a member of American Christian Fiction Writers. When she isn't teaching or writing, she enjoys dates with her husband, shopping trips with her girls, dinners with her best friend and all-night brainstorming with her writing buddies. You can reach her at jenwrites4god@bellsouth.net or jennifercollinsjohnson.com.

Books by Jennifer Collins Johnson

Love Inspired Heartsong Presents

A Heart Healed
A Family Reunited
A Love Discovered
Arizona Cowboy
Arizona Lawman
Arizona Pastor

JENNIFER COLLINS JOHNSON

Arizona Pastor

HEARTSONG
PRESENTS

Recycling programs for this product may not exist in your area.

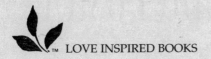 LOVE INSPIRED BOOKS

ISBN-13: 978-0-373-48773-8

Arizona Pastor

www.Harlequin.com

Printed in U.S.A.

A father to the fatherless, a defender of widows
is God in His holy dwelling.
—*Psalms* 68:5

This book is dedicated to an organization
that taught me so much about writing,
American Christian Fiction Writers.

Chapter 1

"No matter what I do, I'll always be a teenage-pregnancy statistic." The words of the midthirties woman on the talk show whirled through Kristy Phillips's mind. She couldn't imagine why the television had been on, but she didn't have time to worry about that now. She was in a hurry. Even if the words hit close to home.

She rummaged through her closet to find something that would look like new for a very special event: her daughter's high school graduation. She settled on a crisp white blouse with a ruffled collar and cuffs and a navy pencil-style skirt, accenting the outfit with oversize, bold green beads she'd discovered on clearance at one of her favorite department stores. In the background all the while was the attractive woman on the screen, close to Kristy's age, wearing a pair of slacks Kristy actually owned and sitting beside a boy—a full-grown boy who was probably very close to Mel's age. Kristy's heart nearly leaped from her chest.

Kristy turned off the television and dumped the contents of one purse into another one. She grabbed her keys off the counter and hustled out the front door. But the woman's words stuck to Kristy like a rayon skirt in need of an antistatic dryer sheet, like gum stuck on the bottom of a new high heel. *I'll always be a teenage-pregnancy statistic. I'll always...*

When she finally arrived at the auditorium where the school was hosting the high school graduation, Kristy hiked her name-brand-knock-off bag higher up on her shoulder. A plastered smile curved her lipstick-covered lips as she made her way through the sea of parents and family members scurrying to find the best seats in the packed place. Uneasiness quickened her heartbeat as she recognized a few of the faces on the stage. Her daughter's principal had been Kristy's principal. The assistant principal had been Kristy's tenth-grade math teacher. Many things had changed, and yet many things had stayed the same. *Of course, eighteen years isn't much time for a complete faculty change.*

No matter what I do, I'll always be a teenage-pregnancy statistic. The words taunted her. She glanced down at her skirt, hoping no one could tell she'd slip stitched a part of the hem, which had come loose on the left side. She'd had the skirt for several years, but it was a classic, never going out of style. Most of Kristy's clothes were of that nature. After finally finding a seat, Kristy nodded to the older woman beside her. "Hello."

"Hello, honey." The woman's white hair was wound in loose curls atop her head. Though wrinkles trekked over the woman's face and neck, her green eyes sparked with lively mischief. "My great-grandson is graduating today. Who are you here for?"

"My daughter, Amelia Adams."

"My, my, but you don't look old enough to have a child graduating high school."

Kristy's smile wavered momentarily. *That's because I'm not.* She blinked the thought away. "Thank you."

The older woman turned toward the teenager sitting beside her, probably another great-grandson. *No matter what I do, I'll always be a teenage-pregnancy statistic.* Kristy let out a long breath, envisioning the much-too-young woman on the television screen no more than two hours before.

Kristy tried to take in her surroundings. Academia was not foreign to her. She'd spent the past ten years teaching freshmen and sophomore English at the local community college. A not-so-glorious position in a not-so-prestigious environment, Kristy was still content with the strides she'd made since having Mel at the young age of just-turned-eighteen. Some people had doubted that she'd ever be able to get her college degree, but Kristy had proved them wrong. God had guided her every step, but Kristy had still worked many long and hard hours to enjoy a modest, yet comfortable life with her only child.

Amid the bustle of graduation, Kristy's gaze kept wandering to the sea of people around her. She assumed it was the English teacher in her, but Kristy always wondered what people were thinking. For the scowlers, had something happened to cause a possible rift in their daily schedule? For the smilers, were they genuinely that happy or putting on a facade? For the harried, were they notoriously late like Kristy? The last thought shifted Kristy's gaze toward the door. Thankful that for once in her life, she had been on time, Kristy noted a frazzled mother with two younger children in tow, scanning the room for open seats.

Kristy found herself looking for a place for the mother and her children, until the glare of a familiar face Kristy hadn't seen in over a decade forced her to sink down in her metal, fold-up chair. With an instantaneous wave of anger and determination, Kristy sat up, pushed her shoulders back and lifted her chin. She forced herself to smile at the owner of the glaring eyes—her old and longtime-retired high school counselor. The woman nodded abruptly, then focused her attention back on the ceremonies.

I'd forgotten that Ms. Judgmental's granddaughter was in Mel's class. It was funny, almost downright amazing, how the woman's descendants could be so different from their grandmother. Maybe it was because the older woman's influence was diluted after Ms. Jent, or Ms. Judgmental as Kristy preferred to think of her, had moved to sunny Florida almost nine years ago. Her granddaughter was one of Amelia's sweetest friends and would probably be surprised at how hard Ms. Jent had been on Mel's mom.

But Kristy wouldn't be able to forget. Had she known the school counselor's opinion—that pregnant girls shouldn't be allowed in regular classes—Kristy would have never confided in her, especially at the end of her senior year. The counselor offered no other alternative for sinful, unmarried teens. Just GED courses. Ms. Jent's efforts had been in vain. Kristy had had only four months of school left when she'd discovered the pregnancy and had been barely showing by the time she'd graduated.

Determined to focus on something else, Kristy gazed at the podium, trying to grasp the words of the class valedictorian. That wasn't easy, either. The young man at the stand had finally grown into his deep, rich voice and out of his acne-ridden face. Despite the improvement in his appearance, Kristy struggled, listening to the words. He and Amelia had fought neck-and-neck through high school to surpass each other in academics. When the points had been tallied, both had shared the same grade-point average. However, much to Kristy's chagrin, Mel had missed the honor of valedictorian by scoring one point lower on her ACT. And for some reason, this high school had never deigned to allow the salutatorian—the second best—to speak, too.

Ugh. Just listen to my attitude, Lord. I can almost taste the ugliness I feel. Resurrected insecurities from Ms. Jent. Frustration with Mel not being valedictorian. She clasped her hands together and placed them on top of her lap, allowing her right, newly manicured thumbnail to gently scratch the side of her left thumb. *Help me think kind thoughts. Help me look at people as You do.*

Slim Jim finally finished. A chorus of applause erupted as he made his way off the stage and into the mound of fifteen hundred soon-to-be graduates sitting at the front of the auditorium. Navy robes and caps adorned with red-and-blue tassels filled the oversize space.

Realizing her hands' nervous motions, Kristy crossed her legs, unclasped her hands and rubbed her clammy palms against the smooth material of her skirt. She reminded herself not to tap her foot as the high school principal made his way to the podium. Kristy watched as Mel's row filtered out of their seats and toward the stage. Mel would be first to receive her diploma.

Kristy snatched a peek at Mel's father, Tim Adams. Leah, Tim's entirely-too-perfect wife of thirteen years, which also made her Mel's stepmom for the same length of time, leaned forward, craning her neck to see over the crowd to find Mel. They'd probably gotten there early, but even that wouldn't have guaranteed a perfect sight line. Their twelve-year-old and seven-year-old sons also strained to get a peek at their "sister."

Kristy bit back a snarl. It wasn't that she begrudged Tim his happiness. Tim had always been a really nice guy, good-looking, too, which was one of the reasons she'd found herself pregnant her senior year of high school. At the same time, she hated that Leah was so good: Martha Stewart, Betty Crocker and June Cleaver all wrapped into one.

Finally, the assistant principal spoke at the podium, introducing the class. His words jumbled in Kristy's mind until she heard the words *Amelia Adams*.

Cheers rang from the lips of Mel's half brothers, but Kristy tuned them out. She watched as her precious one-and-only walked onto the stage. Mel's curly dark brown hair hung in a shiny mass against the navy robe. Mel sported her new glasses and looked every inch like the beautiful, smart young woman she was. Pride enveloped Kristy's heart. *She'll be an excellent lawyer.*

As quickly as Mel walked up on the stage, she walked off. A wave of emotion flowed through Kristy as an instantaneous memory of anxiety flooded her mind. When Kristy had taken those steps off the stage eighteen years before, she had been terrified. Afraid of what would happen to her. Afraid of what would happen to her baby. Ashamed of what she'd done.

Thank You, God, that everything is so different for Mel.

The principal announced the new graduates, and family and friends swarmed the auditorium floor. Wade Mason stepped out of the way of an elderly woman shuffling toward one of them. He spied the young couple who'd sought his assistance only a few days ago. The girl, Mel was her name, waved as she made her way toward him. A bright smile lit her face, and long dark curls bounced below her shoulders. The tall and thin blond kid, Joel, followed behind her.

"Thank you for coming to our graduation ceremony, Pastor Mason."

Wade shook Mel's, then Joel's, hand. "Please, call me Wade. No need for formalities."

Mel giggled. "My mom would keel over if I called our new minister by his first name."

Joel shifted his weight from one foot to the other, then raked his hand through his hair. "Yeah. Gotta show respect and all."

Wade cringed. They seemed like good kids, but obviously not ready for the adult life they'd saddled themselves with.

"There you are." Mel's mother squeezed through the crowd, then wrapped her arms around her daughter.

He'd met Kristy Phillips at the church's welcome party a month ago and he'd noticed her at the services. How could he not? Deep blue eyes above the cutest splattering of freckles pierced through him whenever she looked at him. After that, he avoided eye contact with her every Sunday, when he scanned the crowd while he preached. She was just too distracting.

Kristy released Mel, then offered a tentative hug to Joel as a tall dark-haired man, a petite blonde woman and two preadolescent boys pushed through the crowd, headed for Mel. Joel's mother and his older and heavier look-alike father made their way to them from the side. Wade took another step back to give the families room, then shoved his hands in the front pockets of his khaki pants.

He enjoyed his new pastoral position at the church in Surprise, and yet he'd spent most of the past few evenings praying and stewing over Joel and Mel. He glanced at Kristy, thinking she might be partly to blame for his sidetracked thoughts. He knew he'd have to talk with her, and she distracted him.

She wasn't the only beautiful single woman in his congregation, but there was something about her. Maybe it was the way she carried herself, shoulders back and chin raised. Or how she touched the base of her neck each time she stood to sing. Whatever it was, she made him lose his focus, and he didn't like the feeling one bit.

Noticing him for the first time, she grabbed his hand in hers. "Pastor Mason. How nice of you to come."

Wade tried to ignore the jolt of electricity that shot up his arm and sent his heart pounding. He looked into her eyes and prayed she couldn't see the attraction he felt. "Call me Wade."

He noted a glimmer of interest in her gaze, then she looked away. "I've never called a pastor by his first name."

"You've probably never had a pastor your age."

She gazed back at him, and he felt her scrutiny from his head to his toes. Finally, she smiled, exposing a slight dimple in her left cheek he hadn't noticed before. "I suppose Pastor James might have been a decade or two older than you."

"Or four." Wade dipped his chin and lifted one eyebrow. "Just how old do you think I am?"

"Fifty? Sixty, maybe?"

He raised his eyebrows at her little joke, and she laughed. He shook his head. "No."

"All right, then. I'll call you Wade."

"Pastor Wade—" Mel grabbed his arm "—I want you to meet my dad and stepmom."

He nodded and shook hands with Mel's, then Joel's, families.

Leah wrapped her hand around Tim's arm. "I hope you'll come to our house for the graduation party."

Out of the corner of his eye, Wade saw Kristy stiffen and lift her chin. Surely she didn't still have feelings for Mel's father. But then, why wouldn't she? Years had passed, but she was still single, and they'd had a child together.

"He's already said he would come," said Mel.

"Terrific," responded Tim. "I've got the steaks and chicken marinating."

"And I've got everything else ready," Leah added.

"Thank you for inviting me. I'll be there." Wade looked at Kristy. Some of the color had drained from her cheeks, and he felt a sudden urge to wrap his arms around her and protect her from the trials she faced. And he knew something she didn't: this day was only going to get harder for her.

Chapter 2

Kristy inhaled a deep breath as she balanced the fruit tray on one hand, then pushed the doorbell with the other. *I can do this.* She brushed her tongue against her teeth once again, praying no lipstick was plastered on them. The door opened and Kristy forced a smile that she hoped portrayed genuineness. "Hello, Leah. Thanks so much for having Mel's party here. Our place is so small, and Mel just insisted..."

"No problem." Leah opened the door wide, allowing a tantalizing French-vanilla aroma to escape the house.

As she motioned Kristy inside, a niggling envy crept up Kristy's spine as she took in the spacious foyer and living area. The kitchen opened up on the left, making the area exceptionally grand and ostentatious. Perfect for a large crowd. Kristy slightly lifted the tray and nodded toward a table piled with mountains of finger foods. "Where would you like me to set this?"

"Mel didn't tell me you were bringing anything. Thank

you so much." Leah took the offering from Kristy's hands, setting it beside a watermelon that had been cut to look like a basket, which was filled with luscious-looking fruits of all colors. A much more beautiful display than Kristy could even dream up, let alone create. "Can I get you a drink?"

Kristy's gaze moved to the smaller table, which held soft drinks of all kinds and bottles of water. "I'll just take a water." She scooped one into her hand, unscrewed the top and took a quick drink. "Is Mel here yet?"

"Yes. She and Joel are on the deck with several others. Grab yourself some food and go on out there."

"I might grab a bite to eat in a little bit. But thanks."

Kristy made her way to the back door. She had to hold back a gasp when she walked out onto an oversize deck connected to one of the largest aboveground pools she'd ever seen. The yard was perfectly manicured, with clusters of blackfoot and angelita daisies in various spots along the privacy fence. Finding an open chair, Kristy sat and watched her daughter talk with one of the guests.

Once upon a time, Kristy had dreamed of a home like this, with a husband, a few kids… But there was no point in stewing over things that hadn't happened. People made choices. As a teenager, Kristy had chosen to walk outside God's plan. She'd faced the consequences, but God had still blessed her with Mel. She glanced at her grown child. Mel had the opportunity to do the things God had planned for her. Her whole life was an open slate, ready for God to fill it with His will. Thrill wrapped itself around Kristy as she thought of the potential her girl's life encompassed.

Mel spotted her and waved. "Mom, you're here." Her daughter made her way up the steps of the deck. "Hey, don't leave early. I need to talk with you."

Before Kristy could respond, Mel nodded and waved at another guest who'd just arrived. Though Kristy hadn't seen the woman in years, she appeared to be Tim's mom. Kristy wanted to hide beneath the chair. His mother had never been fond of Kristy after she and Tim had discovered the pregnancy. If only her own parents could have come…or one of her sisters. But that was impossible. Her parents were missionaries in Brazil. Her middle sister was in the military, stationed in Japan, and her youngest sister had just given birth to her first child only three days before and couldn't attend. Even though she missed having most of her family nearby, life had definitely been busy, which was nice. And it kept Kristy from thinking about her daughter's new freedom.

Taking a deep breath, Kristy settled deeper into her chair. She'd just patiently wait out this day. Mel wanted to talk with her. She probably wanted to be sure all her information had been sent to the college.

Kristy watched as Joel walked up beside Mel. He placed his arm around her back. *Ugh.* Kristy hated how serious the two of them had become. Joel was a great kid, but he and Mel had such different goals. He would one day take over the family plumbing business, and she would one day possibly take over a courtroom. Once Mel went to college, she'd find a nice young man with similar likes and dislikes to hers, not someone so clearly opposite. She just needed to keep her good sense intact and not fall too hard for Joel.

It seemed like forever, but at last the crowd started to dwindle, and soon only Tim, Leah, their children and Kristy remained. Then Kristy spied the new pastor and Joel still talking in the far corner of the yard. She shifted in her chair, antsy to head home, but Mel reminded her not to leave.

"I think everyone's gone." Mel walked out onto the deck. Joel and Wade made their way to them. "It's time to talk."

Kristy furrowed her brows. Why were Tim and Leah

and their boys taking seats around the deck? Mel wanted to talk to Kristy. Why would that include everyone? And why were Joel and Wade still here?

Something gripped Kristy's stomach. She hadn't eaten a bite since she'd arrived. Her nerves were in overdrive after spending an entire day at Tim's house. But this feeling seemed to top the hunger and nerves. *Oh, dear God, what is going on?*

Mel nestled closer to Joel, wrapping her arms around one of his. "Mom, Joel and I are getting married." Mel looked at Kristy, then down at her feet. "I'm pregnant."

Kristy jumped out of the chair, causing it to fall backward. "You're what?"

Mel lowered her chin toward her chest, like a scolded puppy, and whispered, "Pregnant."

Shock and disbelief swirled through Kristy's mind. This couldn't be happening. Kristy gripped the deck's post. No. There must be some mistake. Mel was second in her graduating class. She was the best debater on the academic team. She was a brilliant, beautiful young lady who would go to college and experience everything life had to offer. She could not be…

Kristy dug her nails into the wood of the deck as her breathing grew labored. She closed her eyes, begging God to wake her up from this nightmare.

Determined to regain control, Kristy released the death grip on the railing and turned to face her daughter and her boyfriend. "I think I misunderstood. How could it be possible…?"

Mel's courage seemed to return, and she straightened her shoulders and rolled her eyes. "Please, Mom. I think you know about the birds and the bees."

"I know it's a shock, Kristy." Leah's voice sounded from the other end of the deck.

Kristy glared at her daughter's stepmother. Though Kristy strived to be Christian-like, prayed for blessings on the woman—sometimes, at least—she still couldn't stand Leah. Short, choppy perfect-shade-of-blond hair. Complexion so clear and wrinkle-free, she made babes envious. A shape that even women who'd never carried children would die for. And Mel had always idolized her.

Ha! What a joke. Adult life had played out far easier for Leah than anything Kristy had ever known. The woman had a husband who was crazy about her, who wanted her to spend time and money on haircuts and clothes. Leah's only job was to care for her family, a monumental, honorable task, but Kristy had always been forced to hold a job, go to school *and* take care of her family.

Why wouldn't Leah's house be perfect? Why wouldn't she look great?

Why wouldn't Mel want the same thing?

Bile rose in Kristy's throat. She covered her mouth with her hand, willing her insides to stop churning. A sudden thought swept through her mind. She furrowed her brows. *Why doesn't Leah seem shocked by the news?* She glanced at Tim, who stood ramrod straight and still, but whose only expression was to take in Kristy's response. Why didn't Tim seem shocked, either?

She scanned the deck, searching the faces of Tim, Leah, Mel, Joel, the two boys. Even Wade. All of them stared at Kristy. All of them awaited her reaction.

All of them already knew.

Kristy scooped her purse off the floor. "I've got to go."

Before anyone could respond, she raced down the deck's steps, through the gate and to her car. After finding her keys, Kristy unlocked the door and slipped inside. As she started the car, fury overtook the shock. Mel had told them before she'd told Kristy. She'd even told their brand-new pastor before she'd told her mother.

Kristy shook her head. Bewilderment washed through her. When could this have happened? And where? A sick feeling swished through Kristy's stomach. She'd taught a night class on Tuesdays last semester. Surely Mel and Joel weren't… Mel knew she wasn't allowed to have him over if Kristy wasn't there. Kristy pounded the top of the steering wheel. *Just like Tim and I weren't supposed to go to his house when his mom and dad were at work.*

"Dear Lord, my sins have come back to haunt me." Kristy bit the inside of her lip. Afraid of the emotions that were beginning to overwhelm her, she turned the car. She wasn't ready to go home. Pain and disappointment began to settle into her heart. As if of its own volition, the vehicle headed toward her youngest sister Carrie's house. Maybe the full force of it all wouldn't hurt so much if Kristy talked with her sister.

Kristy pulled into the drive and slipped out of the car. Halfway up the sidewalk, she could hear the wails of a newborn. After hurrying the rest of the way, she knocked on the door. Carrie opened it with tears streaming down her face. The front of her shirt was soaked from her chest to her belly.

Pushing her own troubles to the back of her mind, Kristy walked inside, wrapped her sister in a quick hug, then scooped up her wailing nephew from the bassinet. "How can I help?"

Carrie's body shook with sobs. "He's hungry and my milk came in and I'm too full. He can't latch on. And he won't stop crying. And…"

Kristy gently jostled Noah in her arms to calm him. "Where's Michael?"

Carrie pulled at the front of her shirt. "There was a

double homicide and they called him into work and he said he'd hurry but…"

Kristy touched her sister's arm with her free hand. "It's okay. I'm here now. Go change your shirt. Do you remember me showing you how to use the breast pump?"

Carrie nodded. "I've been trying, but Noah's crying has me crying and I can't stop shaking long enough to…"

"It's okay. I've got Noah. Pump a bit. Then I'll help."

Carrie started down the hall, then turned back around. She wiped her swollen eyes with the back of her hand. "I was praying God would send you."

"And He did. Now hurry on back there so we can feed my little nephew."

Kristy turned her attention back to the baby. Noah squirmed in her arms. She grabbed the pacifier from the bassinet and held it in his mouth. Her little sister was twenty-six and had been praying and preparing for a baby for three years, but tonight it was just too much for Carrie to handle.

How could Mel handle this?

A memory Kristy hadn't thought of in years flooded her mind. Mel was only five days old. Kristy had already nursed her, had already changed her diaper, had done everything she knew to do to make Mel content. But she would not stop crying. Exhaustion had made Kristy irrational. The baby would just not settle down. In an instant, less than a second, Kristy had hefted Mel into the air above her head and screamed, "Why won't you stop crying?"

A powerful urge to shake the tears out of Mel had washed in and out of her. The feeling had scared Kristy to her core. She'd gently brought Mel close to her chest as tears had spilled down her cheeks and onto Mel's head. Kristy had never understood how someone could get so angry with a baby, and yet this wretched, horrible feeling had come over her. Kristy had almost shaken Mel…

"But I didn't," she whispered to Noah, then looked up at the ceiling. "Oh, dear Jesus, Mel's too young for this."

With a heavy heart, Wade drove to the small two-bedroom home he'd leased for a year. He'd selected the residence because of the older neighborhood with its large backyards. After parking in the drive, he opened the front door. Bo, his eighty-pound dalmatian, greeted him with a playful bark and wagging tail. Wade bent down and scratched behind the dog's ears, then petted his back. "How you doing, big guy?"

Bo whined, then barked a response as he ran toward the back door. Wade tossed the car keys on the counter, grabbed a water bottle out of the refrigerator, then let him out. He sat on a lounge chair as Bo raced around the yard. Leaning back, he closed his eyes and allowed the sun to warm his face. He prayed for Mel and Joel, but especially for Kristy.

Why had Mel and Joel told her that way? In front of Tim and Leah and their sons? Wade had thought that the couple might have wanted moral support as they told the whole family, but he'd soon discovered that Kristy alone had been the one to receive the graduation surprise.

He scrunched his nose as he tried to imagine how he would feel. Ironically, his sermon the next day was about communication with our Christian brothers and sisters. He trailed his hand down the front of his face. He'd need to look over the scriptures once more before going to bed.

Sitting forward in the chair, he released a long sigh. He'd forgotten to stop by the church and pick up his laptop after the graduation party. He stood and whistled to Bo. "You wanna go for a ride?"

Bo barked and jumped. He loved to go anywhere Wade would take him. Once in the car, Wade rolled down the passenger window and Bo stuck out his head. The dog seemed to smile against the wind as Wade drove to the church. He powered up all the windows halfway, then raced into his office, grabbed his laptop and made it back to the car in less than a few minutes.

Knowing Bo would enjoy a walk around the church's extensive property, he hooked the leash to Bo's collar and opened the car door. Between the early-morning sermon preparations, the graduation ceremony and the party, Wade needed a walk, as well.

Shoving his keys into his pocket, he headed toward the bass pond at the edge of the church's property. Having ministered for seventeen years to a smaller congregation in a house of worship with little land, in a metropolitan area, Wade found the several acres his new church owned not only inviting but spiritually stimulating.

Though the land was dry, brown desert more than anything else, a man couldn't take in the oversize sycamore tree or look at the rolling majesty of the White Tanks Mountains and not give credit to his Maker. At the pond, Bo barked, then lapped up a drink of water. Wade sat on one of the few benches dotted around the perimeter. He tried to shake off his concern for Kristy and bask in the closing of the day.

"'Holy, holy, holy is the Lord Almighty, the whole earth is full of his glory.'" Wade quoted from Isaiah the words of the seraphim who circle God's throne. He gazed at the water, which had just an occasional bubble from the bouncing of some small insect. "How could anyone deny You, Lord?"

Taking a deep breath, he felt his heartbeat slow at the natural peace and tranquility of the place. He closed his eyes, lifting his face toward the heavens. "Thank You for bringing me here. I've never felt more confirmed in Your calling."

As quickly as the praise slipped from his lips, he felt a twist in his heart. Loneliness. His relationship with the Lord was good. At least, he thought it was good, but his body, his mind and his heart yearned for more. For years, he'd been content to throw himself into the lives of his flock, but lately, maybe it was because he'd just turned the big four-oh, Wade yearned for more. An image of Kristy slipped through his mind, and he pushed it away.

He thought he'd healed from the death of his father from congestive heart failure five years ago and his mom three years before that to cancer. He was faithful in visiting his sister and her family in Colorado whenever he had a chance, and though he wouldn't consider them close in the sense they didn't talk every night or even every week, he loved and prayed daily for his sibling and her family. Already, he'd been invited to dinner at several of the church members' homes, and there were a few men he knew would be excellent accountability partners. But he felt discontent.

He stood, stretching his arms over his head. Maybe he was just working too hard. Thinking too hard about young pregnant couples and beautiful single women. The land around him shouted of God's glory, and his mind and heart nearly burst with the excitement and peace he felt for his new flock, but he hadn't exercised as he should. He hadn't allowed himself to sleep or even rest as much as a body needed. Maybe that was the only thing wrong with him.

"With that in mind…" He picked up a small, smooth stone and skipped it across the top of the water. Bo barked and raced to the water's edge. "Bo, I think it's time we head home."

He turned and walked the trail back toward the church. He frowned when he noticed a car in the parking lot. The hour was late, and he didn't feel comfortable leaving someone alone. No doubt one of the members was doing last-minute Sunday-school preparations or something of the sort. As long as more than one person was there, he'd feel okay about moving on.

He hooked Bo's leash to the front steps' railing, then grabbed the doorknob and twisted. It was unlocked. He sighed, wishing people would be more careful. Possibly he was more paranoid than necessary, as the outskirts of Surprise were nothing like the heart of Phoenix, but crime still happened here. The fact that the church was a bit secluded, just under a mile from town, also made it an easy target.

"Hello," he called as he walked through the foyer. Opening the sanctuary door, he watched as a familiar-looking woman kneeling in front of the altar jumped up and turned to face him. Wade's heart skipped as he stared at Kristy Phillips. He was a preacher, but he was still a man, a single man. The woman's soft shoulder-length brown hair shone, and her light blue eyes seemed to follow him everywhere. "I'm...I'm so sorry," she stammered, and pressed the front of her skirt. "I thought I was... I didn't think anyone was here."

Her anxious gestures touched him, and he again fought the urge to wrap her in his arms and assure her all was well. He lifted his hand instead. "It's not a problem. Tell you what. I'll wait outside until you're ready to go. I don't want you to be alone."

Kristy gasped, and her entire countenance seemed to crumble. "I've never been so alone in my life."

Chapter 3

Kristy inwardly chastised her wayward emotions. Her eyes and lungs disobeyed her, and tears spilled down her cheeks and she heaved to catch her breath. It was too much. The day had been too much. And now, before the altar of her Heavenly Father and the pastor she'd spoken only a few words to, Kristy's entire being crumbled. The guilt was too heavy. The sadness too deep. The disappointment too maddening.

Hope had fled from her.

Reaching for the front pew, Kristy attempted to control the onslaught of sobs. Her legs shook as she turned herself around and sat down on the padded seat. She wiped her eyes and cheeks. Trying to straighten her shoulders, she found the effort was too much, and she stayed slumped over, staring at the carpet. "I apologize," she mumbled as more tears fell. "I'll just be…a minute."

She didn't look up, but she knew he was there. She could feel his closeness for several seconds before he sat beside her, placed a tissue in one of her hands and grabbed and held on to the other. "How can I help? I'll pray."

His voice was soft and tender but a bit shaky and unsure. He probably wasn't used to seeing grown women have complete meltdowns in front of him. But the comfort of his touch brought a new onset of emotion and renewed tears. Kristy shook her head, unable to say a word.

Embarrassment mingled with the utter defeat and disappointment that overwhelmed her. Her eyes, nose and chest hurt from the physical display of her inner torment.

But he never let go of her hand.

When the tears could no longer flow and her body seemed void of all ability to show emotion, she looked up at the pastor. His deep blue eyes spoke of sincere compassion and concern, causing a new wave of mortification. Noting the stubbles along the strong line of his jaw and the slight cleft in his chin, Kristy wondered if she'd lost her senses completely. "I'm sorry. I'll go now."

Before she could get up, he squeezed her hand. "Is there any way I can help?"

Kristy stared at his hand, much bigger and stronger than hers. For an instant, she thought of God's hand and how He could hold all her troubles, if she'd allow Him. Whether because of a moment of weakness or a nudging from the Lord, Kristy didn't know, but she threw her pride behind her. "I don't know what to do." She pulled her hand from his and smacked it down on the pew. "I've walked this road, and I wanted so much more for Mel. She's got so much potential."

"I know. When she and Joel talked with me—"

"That boy is going to be a plumber, for crying out loud." Kristy dipped her chin, knowing she sounded like a snob and feeling ashamed. His family had helped her on a few occasions. His parents were two of the sweetest people she knew, and there was nothing dishonorable about the occupation. She shook her head at her words and thoughts. *Forgive me, Lord. I am being prideful and arrogant.*

Kristy looked up at her pastor. "That was a terrible thing to say."

"It's okay. You're hurt and venting." He pointed to his chest and grinned. "I'm the right person to do that with."

"Thank you, Wade."

His gaze penetrated hers. Out of seemingly nowhere, an old children's tune flowed through Kristy's mind and she found herself "wading" through Jordan's waters. And, wow, how she could get lost in the blue current of his eyes. She pushed the thought away. "Wade, they're so young."

"But they've made a very grown-up choice. And they were also adult enough to ask me to counsel them before they said their vows."

"They did?" Kristy clasped her hands in her lap. That was good. A mature step in the right direction. She stood up. A small weight lifted, and she determined to cling to it with all she had. "Thanks so much."

On impulse, she wrapped her arms around him. Having hugged her old pastor, a now retired eighty-year-old man, several times, she hadn't prepared herself for Wade's shoulders to be so wide and firm. She hadn't anticipated that he would smell of an intriguing musk. She hadn't expected a charge of electricity to shoot through her. Releasing him quickly, she dipped her head. Without making eye contact again, she turned and headed toward the door.

With the entrance shut firmly behind the woman, Wade scratched the side of his head. "So much for peace and serenity."

He slammed his frame back down onto the pew and stared at the large wooden cross that hung on the wall behind the podium. "What have I gotten myself into, Lord? I was already wrestling with worry over counseling the young couple. And now Kristy…"

He allowed his words to taper off as he studied the dark wood of the cross, noting small places of imperfection where the stain was too dark or too light. He'd pastored a church for years. He knew his job—preach, encourage, guide, serve, minister—and he did all those things…just not the marriage counseling. Until now.

He growled. This time of year was already hard enough. With the resurrection of perennials, fruits and other foliage came the twenty-year-old memories of Zella. To most people, spring was a rejuvenating time of rebirth. To Wade, it was a time of renewed guilt.

Zella had loved the spring. She'd wanted to be married at their home church in that season. It had been all she'd talked about. And he'd loved to hear her talk about their wedding, because when she had, she'd been unable to stop smiling. Though not classically pretty, it'd been her smile that had drawn him. Her smile hadn't been subtle, but rather, it had encompassed her whole face, like a light shining in a dark room. Her optimism had been contagious and had had a way of making the worst of situations all better. She'd been like a comforting balm of aloe on a burn. He'd never forget her.

And he'd never forget what he'd done.

Wade jumped up from the pew. He shouldn't have agreed to counsel that young couple. He should have told them… Clenching his jaw, he shook his head. Turning forty must have played a few tricks on him. A younger Wade never would have taken a job that included counseling couples, especially young, excited, we'll-conquer-the-world-together couples.

That's because it's time to deal with this.

Wade shook the thought away. His sister had said something of that nature the last time he'd visited her. But she didn't understand. She hadn't been there when the accident had happened. She hadn't been the one speeding. God had forgiven him, and to a degree, he had forgiven himself, but he could never forget. Never wanted to forget.

Not forget. Truly forgive and move forward.

Wade scooped his keys out of his front pocket. Fatigue was jumbling his thoughts, messing with his emotions. He had been sure this move, one he'd prayed would be his last, would take his mind off the past pain. Maybe he was just tired. The day had been long and exhausting. He needed to head home and get some rest before preaching in the morning. He walked out the front door, then turned and twisted the knob. Locked. *Just like my heart.*

Chapter 4

Kristy looked at the alarm clock. Between guilt-ridden thoughts and prayers of mercy, she'd barely slept a moment. After forcing herself out of bed, she staggered to the bathroom and splashed cold water on her face. She wiped it dry, then looked at her blotchy, puffy-eyed reflection. She'd hoped someone would call and say the news had been a joke, a high school prank, but the only text she'd received was one from Mel, saying she was spending the night with her dad and Leah. Again.

While Kristy brushed her teeth, she thought of Leah's knowing, pitying expression when Mel had told Kristy about the pregnancy. Jealousy swelled within her. Leah had known everything. Mel had confided in her stepmom, but not Kristy. In Mel's eyes, Leah was understanding and compassionate. Ha. Leah had no idea what being a teen mom was like. She and Tim had both had their degrees and bought a house before they'd got married and had their first son. Sure Tim had already had Mel, and he'd been a good enough dad to her, but he hadn't been the one who'd stayed up all night when she'd had a stomach bug, then had taken college exams the next day. He hadn't been the one who'd begged friends to babysit when professors hadn't allowed a baby in their classes.

Kristy put on a T-shirt and a pair of shorts, then plodded into the kitchen and poured a bowl of cereal and a glass of orange juice. The front door opened as she sat down. "I'm home, Mom" echoed down the hall, and Kristy closed her eyes and asked God to give her the right words to say.

Mel walked into the kitchen and offered a sheepish grin. She tapped the corner of her eye. "Rough night, huh?"

"Just a bit," Kristy responded through clenched teeth.

Mel opened the cabinet. "I'm hungry, but I'm so nauseous. Nothing sounds good." She took a sleeve of crackers from the box and sat down across from Kristy. "Leah tried to give me some eggs and sausage." She crinkled her nose. "But the smell was killing me. Had to get out of there."

Kristy glanced at her bowl of sweetened corn flakes. She wasn't the least bit surprised Leah fed Tim a perfect hot breakfast each morning. "How long have you known about the pregnancy?"

"No beating around the bush, huh?"

Kristy shook her head. She had no desire to play games. Joel and Mel had thrown a curveball into the plan, and now they needed to figure out how to get back on track.

"A month."

Kristy gawked at her daughter. "A month? Mel, we need to make you an appointment with the doctor. Make sure everything is okay."

"Leah's already taken me to her doctor once." She stared

down at the crackers, then shrugged. "She was a nice lady. Got me some prenatal vitamins."

Kristy swallowed back the hurt that threatened to spew from her mouth like an erupting volcano. How could Mel trust her stepmom more than her? Kristy had been the one to care for Mel when she'd been sick, to run to the store for materials for last-minute homework assignments, to go to concerts and parent/teacher conferences and host birthday parties. She'd thought they were as close as peanut butter and jelly. She cleared her throat. "When's your due date?"

"January 13."

Kristy cringed. "Beginning of spring semester. But at least you'll be able to get half a year under your belt."

"I'm not going to school in the fall."

"Don't worry. Fall won't be a problem. You might be a little physically uncomfortable by the end of the semester, but—"

"I'm not going at all next year."

Kristy stared at her daughter, noting her set jaw and defensive posture.

"Now, Mel—"

"Mom, I don't want to be a lawyer. I haven't wanted to be a lawyer for two years. I've tried to tell you, but you'd never listen."

"Okay." Kristy placed her spoon in the cereal bowl, willing herself to remain calm. "But you still need to get a degree."

"Why? I want to be a wife and mom and maybe teach piano and guitar lessons on the side."

"Well, Mel. I know you love your music, and you think Joel will be with you forever—"

"Just because you didn't want to be with Dad doesn't mean things won't work out for me and Joel."

Kristy wiped her palms against her shorts. "Honestly, Mel. You are smarter than this. I've raised you—"

"You've raised me to be independent, to take care of myself, but I'm choosing to trust God."

Kristy huffed. "Really? I'm pretty sure the Bible has a few things to say about waiting for intimacy until you're married."

"This is why I didn't come to you first." Mel hopped out of the chair. "We messed up, but we're trying to make it right."

The doorbell rang before Kristy could blast her with a retort of how foolish and immature she and Joel had been.

"Who's that?" Mel asked.

"Probably Carrie. I'm watching Noah so she and Michael can have lunch together."

Mel's eyes glistened as Kristy hustled to the front door. Kristy huffed. Maybe spending some time with her fussy nephew would help her see just how challenging life would be for her and Joel.

She could hear Noah's cries, even before opening the front door. Carrie's eyes were puffier than Kristy's, and exhaustion marked her features. She offered a weak smile. "He's hungry. Doc took him off the soy-formula supplement. Now we're trying a superexpensive brand that's supposed to be close to breast milk."

Carrie placed the car seat on the coffee table, and Kristy hoisted Noah out of the seat, then bounced around to calm him.

"No problem. Why don't you take a good nap before you come back to get him?"

"You mean it?"

"Absolutely. My day is open, and you look tired."

"I am worn out. We're just having such a hard time figuring out what his digestive system can tolerate." She exhaled a long breath, then turned to Mel. "I'm sorry I missed your graduation party." She wrapped her arms around her. "I'm so proud of you."

Kristy shooed her sister out the door. "Go on and get some lunch and rest."

"Okay." She waved, then winked at Mel. "Enjoy the peaceful years now." She nodded to Noah. "Everything changes when you have a baby."

Kristy almost laughed out loud at her sister's advice, but Noah released a scream that echoed through the house. She handed Mel the baby, then searched through the diaper bag for the bottle. She placed the bottle in a cup of warm water, then went back to the living room to take the screaming infant from her daughter. Mel's perplexed expression said it all. She wasn't ready to be a mother.

After an early-morning run with Bo, during which Wade had thought about the sermon he'd preached last Sunday on God's grace in the midst of trials, he still felt conflicted about counseling Mel and Joel. Not to mention Kristy's continual invasion into his thoughts. She'd sat stoically through the church service, with Mel and Joel beside her holding hands. Tonight, after the midweek prayer meeting, the church would recognize the graduates, and Wade felt anxious for Kristy all over again.

"Here ya go, Pastor Wade." Eustace Owens, one of the church's active senior citizens, handed him a grouping of three balloons. She pointed to the corner. "If you wouldn't mind, tape those up there. I'm not quite as sturdy on a ladder as I used to be."

"Of course." Wade took the balloons and secured them. "You all have done a terrific job." He looked at each of the four women, who were decorating the church's fellowship hall. "Last spring we recognized graduates at my church in Phoenix, but nothing this elaborate."

"Doesn't take much to get us excited about celebrating," said Ida Freemont, the oldest lady of the bunch, though he'd have never known it if she hadn't said as much. She wore her hair to her shoulders and kept it dyed to a dark brown. Her clothes and even her glasses were trendy, not so much as to appear tacky, but she definitely seemed a few decades younger than her age.

"We like to eat," added Dortha Evans.

"And compete to see who makes the best dishes," Eustace piped in.

"Not me." Wilma Rice snorted. "We all know I can't cook."

The women mumbled their agreement.

Wilma continued, "But I make sure drinks and paper products are available."

"And you're the kindest of all of us." Dortha wrapped her arm around Wilma.

Eustace huffed and then rolled her eyes as she turned back to Wade. "Here's how this works. You'll do a ten- or fifteen-minute devotional about the graduates starting new lives. Then we'll give them their gifts—a new Bible, a framed certificate and a gift card to a department store. One of the deacons will say a prayer over the food and then we'll eat. Okay?"

Wade bit his tongue at Eustace's abrasive orders. He hadn't been here long enough to force changes on the congregation, but he also didn't like being told how to lead a recognition service. Still, to keep the peace and in an effort to gain their trust, he would go along with her demanding ways. For now. He clasped his hands together. "That sounds fine. We have twelve graduates?"

"Yes. Four from college. Two more who are graduating from college, but they were nontraditional students, already have kids. The other six are all from high school. Two were taught at home. The other four attended different schools. Except Mel and Joel. They went to the same one."

Wade nodded. A scowl furrowed Eustace's brows, and she leaned closer to him. "I've heard rumors about Mel and Joel."

The other ladies heard Eustace and dropped their decorations and walked toward them.

"Don't start with that," said Ida. "That's just a bunch of gossip."

"You're the one who told me," retorted Eustace.

"I know, but I should have kept my mouth shut." Ida shook her head.

Wilma clicked her tongue. "Kristy would be devastated." She placed her palm on her chest. "If the rumor's true, I mean."

"The poor dear has worked so hard all these years," added Dortha.

"These days, kids do whatever they want to do," said Eustace. "And let's be honest. It would serve Kristy right."

Wade fought back the desire to put the elderly woman in her place. He wasn't sure what rumor they'd heard, but whether true or not, Eustace obviously hadn't listened to his sermon about God's grace through trials.

"Now, Eustace," Wilma cooed. "Didn't you listen to Pastor Wade talk about God's grace?"

He bit back a grin. The woman must have been a mind reader.

"Of course God gives us grace," Eustace retorted. "But He also says He punishes children to the third and fourth generation when we don't follow His laws."

"Oh, dear." Ida pressed her fingertips against her mouth.

Wade couldn't keep silent any longer. "I'm not sure

what rumor you've heard, but no matter what they have or haven't done, God loves a repentant heart. He blesses us when we acknowledge our sins and turn back to Him."

"Sure." Eustace bristled. "But we still gotta face the consequences."

Wilma waved her hand through the air. "Stop all this, Eustace. If the rumor is true, we'll be doing more celebrating."

"Like a wedding and a baby shower," Eustace snapped, then turned toward him. "I also heard you're going to be doing some marriage counseling."

Wade had no idea who had shared all this information with Eustace. Everything she said was true, but she made the circumstances sound as if they'd been secretive and sinful. Joel and Mel should not have gotten pregnant. They should have waited before having a physical relationship. But they hadn't. They were repentant and looking toward following God now. They couldn't change the past, but they could press on and fight the good fight for the future.

He churned over a response in his mind. He'd dealt with many hardened, bitter or judgmental members in his old congregation, where he'd ministered for seventeen years. Often their attitudes had stemmed from their own needs for forgiveness, and they'd sought to hurt others as a ruse. Remembering this, his heart softened for the woman, and he smiled. "Eustace, I can't tell you the private information about other members, but you can pray. When you hear something about one of your brothers or sisters, pray that God will heal and bless them."

"Humph." Eustace picked up several tablecloths and headed toward the other side of the fellowship hall. Her friends joined her, and then they spread them on the tables.

Wade focused on getting chairs out of the storage closet and setting them up around the tables. Just like any family, every church had people who thrived on stirring discord. *God, show me how to be a leader. How to lead by example. Right now, I don't feel love for Eustace. I feel a need to show her the sin of gossip in Your word, to show her how You loved the unlovable.*

As the prayer slipped through his mind, he looked over at the women. They cackled as they pressed the creases with their hands. Eustace saw Kristy and Mel and Joel as unlovable. He saw Eustace as the unlovable one. If he was going to lead by example, he'd have to purposefully choose to love Eustace.

Chapter 5

In no time at all, Kristy stood outside Tim and Leah's home once again. She glanced back at the driveway. Joel's truck was here, as was his parents' car. The new pastor parked his truck in front of the house. Then he and an oversize dalmatian hopped out of the front seat. A leash kept the excited canine from barreling toward her. Wade waved with his free hand. "Thought I was gonna be late."

"You're talking about wedding plans with us?"

He shrugged. "I guess so. They wanted me to come with my calendars, the church's and my own." He leaned toward her, and she caught a quick whiff of musky cologne. "Though my personal calendar is pretty much the same as the church's."

A wave of relief washed over Kristy that she wouldn't be alone for the meeting. Not that Wade was *with* her. He just kind of evened the playing field of married people and single people. Not that there was a playing field to begin with. She had no reason to compare herself to Tim's perfect homemaker of a wife or to Joel's parents, Chuck and Mary, who'd been happily married for more than a quarter of a century. She swallowed back a sigh, hating the inferiority complex that always wrapped around her when she was near Tim and Leah.

Kristy glanced down at Wade's dog. The big guy shook his bottom from side to side and bobbed his nose in an attempt to get her attention. She offered her hand for the canine to sniff, then petted the top of his head. "What's his name?"

"Knew he was a boy, did you?"

She smiled. "You just don't look like a girl-dog kind of guy."

Wade laughed, and Kristy couldn't help but giggle at the boisterous sound. "His name is Bo." He scratched behind the dog's ears. "Tim said he could come over and run around the backyard and keep the boys occupied while we talk."

Kristy nodded and straightened to her full height. "Guess we should go ahead and get in there."

"Have you knocked or rang the doorbell?"

She scrunched her nose and shook her head.

"I'll do it, then."

He pushed the bell, and within a moment, Leah answered, looking perfect and flashing a bright white smile. Wade placed his hand in the small of Kristy's back and guided her inside. Kristy held her breath at his touch. She'd lived independently and alone for so long, she couldn't remember when someone had led her anywhere. Part of her kind of liked the feeling.

"You can head to the dining room, Kristy." Leah pointed to her left. "I took the liberty of purchasing a few bridal magazines. Mel and Mary are already perusing them while the guys talk baseball." She laughed, a light tinkling sound that grated on Kristy's nerves.

"The boys are in the back," she addressed Wade. "They can't wait to meet your dog. What did you say his name was again?" Leah's words drifted off as she and Wade walked to the back of the house.

Once in the dining room, Kristy's heart twisted at the vision of Mel and Mary scouring bridal magazines. Dark curly locks fell past Mel's shoulders. With no makeup to cover them, freckles splattered her cheeks and nose. If Kristy had a couple of ponytail holders, she could put Mel's hair in pigtails and her child would look just as she had in elementary school.

The guys sat at the other end of the table, oblivious to Mel and Mary's discussion. Her future son-in-law's blond hair swept down in waves almost to his eyebrows and past his ears. He didn't look much older than a middle-school boy in need of a haircut.

Lord, they have no idea what they're getting into. I wanted so much more for Mel.

As if sensing her prayer, Mel glanced up and offered a tentative smile. She motioned Kristy to a place beside her. Trying to maintain a positive demeanor, Kristy sat down and looked at the long, straight dress she and Mary had found. "I'd like to find something like this."

"That would look beautiful on your slim figure," said Mary.

"Won't be slim for long," Kristy muttered, then wished she could take back the words when she saw hurt in Mel's eyes.

"I shouldn't be showing much by the end of July. Lots of women are still small at sixteen weeks."

"July?" Kristy interrupted. Her voice raised an octave. "Have you lost your mind?"

The room fell silent as the guys turned and stared at her. Tim seemed to hold his breath. Joel leaned closer to his dad, who looked down at his hands.

"No, Mom," Mel whipped out. "We're not crazy."

Leah and Wade walked into the room. They seemed to sense the tension as they looked at each of them. Leah sat beside Tim, which meant Wade had no choice but to sit beside Kristy. Ignoring the thrill that shot through her at his nearness, Kristy fired back, "Where do you plan to live?"

Leah took Tim's hand and crossed her long, toned and tanned legs. "My parents own some rental property. It just so happens they have a small two-bedroom house that will be available the first of July. Of course they're going to give their only granddaughter reduced rent until she and Joel get on their feet."

Their only granddaughter. The words sliced through Kristy like a knife through soft butter. "Even reduced rent costs." She looked from Mel to Joel. "Just how do you intend to pay your bills?"

Chuck cleared his throat. "Joel's gonna be working for me full-time, starting this week. He's already registered for his training. Always planned to take over my business one day."

"And I've got a couple of kids signed up to take piano lessons," said Mel as she lifted her hand. "And before you say anything, they're going to come here, to Dad's house, until we get a piano set up in our place." She glanced at Joel with a look full of love and adoration.

Kristy didn't want to be the bad guy, but they needed to understand this whole situation would be much more challenging than they expected. Things wouldn't simply fall into place for eighteen-year-old, barely-out-of-high-school parents. She opened her mouth, but Tim spoke first.

"Before you say it, Mel and the baby will be able to be on my insurance until Joel is able to take some out for the family. I've already checked."

She pinched her lips together. They'd all thought of just everything. What about the fact that they were too young, that Mel had the brains, the potential to take any career path she wanted? She glanced from Mel to Joel again, imploring them to see reason. "A month and a half is so fast. Don't you two want to take a little time? Make sure this is the right choice."

"I don't want to be showing when I walk down the aisle," Mel huffed, and crossed her arms.

Well, that just proved her maturity. Kristy had heard the same tone and witnessed the same motion every time her daughter threw a tantrum as a child. And given how frazzled her daughter had been with Noah the week before, she definitely needed practice with babies.

Joel cleared his throat, but his voice still squeaked when he spoke. "We don't want to upset you, Ms. Phillips, but Mel and I want to go ahead and get married."

Mel curled her lip. "Besides, I'm almost eighteen, and I can do—"

Joel placed his hand on Mel's arm. "We want you to be part of this with us."

Kristy pursed her lips. She had to give the boy credit for his effort in keeping peace between her and Mel.

He offered a quick nod. "Pastor Wade," Joel said, "we're hoping for July 27. Does that date work for you?"

"What?" Kristy slapped her palms on the table and implored her child. "What about Grandma and Grandpa and Aunt Kaitlyn? They won't be able to see you get married."

"Maybe they can work something out," Mel said. "It's the date Joel and I want to have, and the wedding is about us."

A wave of nausea swept through Kristy. What had happened to the daughter she was so proud of? She sounded like a spoiled brat and not the way Kristy had raised her. She was still waiting to awaken from this nightmare or for someone to jump out from behind a wall and shout that the whole thing was some kind of prank.

"That date should be fine," responded Wade.

Guess not, Kristy inwardly retorted. For years, Mel had been her whole world. Now Kristy watched as her life was about to crash and burn before her eyes.

Wade opened the day on his smartphone's calendar. "What time were you thinking?"

"It'll be super hot," said Mel, "so I'm thinking in the evening."

"We have to do it on the half hour so the time is going up when you say your vows," said Leah.

Kristy rolled her eyes, and Wade cleared his throat. "So six-thirty or seven-thirty?"

"Seven-thirty is probably better." Mel looked at Joel. "I know we'll need to get up early the next morning for the cruise—"

Kristy lifted her hand. "Wait a minute. What? You're already going on a cruise?"

"Yes." Mel clapped her hands.

"That's why we were hoping the twenty-seventh worked for Pastor Wade," added Joel.

Mel glanced over at her future in-laws with adoration gleaming in her eyes. "Chuck and Mary surprised us last night. Said they wanted to be sure we had a honeymoon."

Chuck put his arm around Mary. "We married pretty young. Never had a chance to get away."

Mary shrugged. "We figured since we have the means,

we ought to make sure the kids get some time together before the baby comes."

Kristy's face paled as her gaze went from one couple to the other. Wade knew she felt like an outsider, with Joel and Mel, Chuck and Mary and Tim and Leah all holding hands or leaning into each other. He felt a bit awkward himself.

Kristy grinned, but the tightness in her jaw belied the effort. "That's terrific."

To change the subject, Wade said, "We'll need to set up the four marriage-counseling sessions." His gut twisted at the idea.

"Let's set up one a week, starting this week. That will leave the last couple weeks open for wedding errands," said Joel.

Mel leaned over and kissed his cheek. "My fiancé is so sensitive. You're going to be the best husband ever."

Kristy stiffened. As a reflex, Wade patted her arm. She looked at him, her gaze imploring him to see her side. He did understand, and at that moment, he wanted to wrap his arms around her and comfort her.

They settled on the dates for the counseling sessions. Then Leah showed a picture of a dish in one of the magazines. "This potato casserole looks delicious. Maybe we could serve it at the reception."

"I was thinking more along the lines of finger foods," said Kristy. "Or maybe even just cake and punch."

"Cake and punch? Mom, really?" Mel grunted. "Nobody does that anymore."

Kristy's face blazed red. "I'm just thinking we should be economical about this. We don't have much time, and—"

"Don't worry about money at all," Leah chimed in as she squeezed her husband's arm. "Tim and I are going to pay for the wedding."

Kristy shook her head. "No."

"We insist. We already discussed it last night. She's our only girl…"

Kristy's body went ramrod straight, and Wade watched her suck in her breath and ball her fists. This planning session needed to end, and fast.

She slammed her palms on the table. "Sounds as though you all have everything planned. I wonder why you bothered to invite me."

Leah placed her palm on her chest. "Well, of course Mel wants her mother to be here." She glanced at Tim, her expression full of innocence.

Before Kristy could say anything more, Wade grabbed her hand and squeezed it. She jerked toward him. Her eyes flashed, and for a moment, he feared she'd unleash a flurry of angry words at him. He held tight to her hand as he said, "I have a few questions about the church's monthly newsletter." He looked around at expressions that seemed to fear her fury as much as he did.

Looking back into Kristy's glare, he willed back his confidence. Deep blue eyes screamed embarrassment and pain. "I hate to tear you away, but could I get your help for a half hour or so? I need to have it completed by tomorrow."

Kristy's shoulders fell. "Sure."

Wade addressed Leah and Tim. "This shouldn't take long. Would you mind if Bo stayed until I bring Kristy back?"

Leah waved her hand. "Absolutely. The boys are enjoying their new playmate. We might have to borrow him from time to time."

Trying to quickly get her out of the house, Wade nodded as he stood. "We'll figure something out."

Kristy took a step toward the door, then turned and wrapped her arms around Mel. She didn't say a word, just hugged her child, then headed outside. Wade prayed for guidance as he followed the beguiling woman to the truck. He also had to think about what exactly he should ask her.

Chapter 6

Wade tapped the top of the steering wheel and tried to focus on the contemporary Christian music filling the cab of his truck. Years had passed since he'd felt jittery driving with a lovely woman in the passenger seat. He wrinkled his nose. In truth, he hadn't chauffeured any women for a very long time. Unless he counted his mom. Or his sister. But jitters never accompanied him when he rode with them. Unless they were driving.

He sneaked a quick glance at Kristy. Her lips were pursed so tight that wrinkles covered her chin. She blinked several times, but he still spied the tears threatening to spill over her lids.

"Thanks for getting me out of there," she whispered.

"You're welcome."

The words proved too much for her because she gasped. Then tears streamed down her cheeks. Wade glanced around the cab until he spied an unused napkin from a fast-food restaurant. She nodded her thanks when she took it, and he again tried to focus on the road. One of his favorite songs about God's amazing love wafted from the speakers, and he silently prayed she would drink in the words and allow them to be a healing balm to her heart.

She sniffed. "Do you really have a newsletter question for me?"

He did have one question, though he'd planned to ask Chad, the music minister, or Greg, the youth minister, but Kristy would be a better choice. "I do need some advice."

Sneaking a peek at her, he winked. The smile she gave him lit up her face and made her already-glistening eyes sparkle. "But I probably didn't have to steal you away to ask it."

She giggled, and Wade's heart flipped. He pulled into the parking lot of Paradise Bakery and Café.

"So what's your question?"

He parked, then shifted in his seat to face her. "I'm going to add a short devotional to the newsletter." He cupped his chin with his thumb and pointer finger, then tapped his jaw. "Do you think I should do that at the beginning or end?"

Kristy dipped her chin and narrowed her eyelids. "That's your question?"

"It's a question." He motioned to her. "You're the English professor. I was going to ask Chad or Greg, but you'd definitely have the most professional opinion."

She grinned, then tilted her head. "Okay. I'd say at the beginning. Put everyone in a God-centered frame of mind before they start reading."

"Sounds like a terrific idea," he agreed. "Actually, that's perfect."

She furrowed her brows. "You doubted me?"

"Not for a moment."

She motioned to the café. "So why did we come here?"

"Thought we'd get a cup of coffee, maybe say a prayer to help you feel less bamboozled."

"What if I don't drink coffee?"

Wade scoffed. "A teacher who doesn't drink coffee?"

Kristy laughed, all evidence of tears gone. "I'm kidding. Of course I do."

They got out of the truck and walked into the café. Kristy ordered a caramel latte and a scone, while he got a black decaf and a cinnamon roll. He found a place in the corner, surrounded by windows. She took a sip of her latte, then stared at him.

He wiped his mouth, then looked down to see if he had cinnamon-and-sugar crumbs splattered across his shirt. "What?"

The left corner of her lips curled up. "Bamboozled, huh?"

"Impressed by my vocabulary?"

She shook her head. "Not a word I hear every day."

"Maybe I'm smarter than the people who you come into contact with."

"With whom you come into contact."

"Excuse me?"

"If you're going to impress the English professor, you shouldn't end your sentence with a preposition."

"What's a preposition?"

"With."

"With what?"

Kristy leaned back in her chair and laughed, a deep, to-the-bottom-of-her-belly sound. Wade joined in her mirth as he searched his mind for the meaning of *preposition*. He remembered learning the word and that his teacher had connected it to a mouse going places. That was all his discombobulated mind could recall. He sat up. Maybe he'd have a chance to throw out that word, as well.

She finished the last bite of her scone as he swallowed the last of his coffee. A chuckle slipped through her lips, and she exhaled a breath. "Thanks, Wade."

He lifted one eyebrow. "Feeling less discombobulated?"

She laughed again. "Not if you don't stop using big words."

"Was that a double negative I just heard?"

She scooped up her trash, then grabbed his hand. "Come on. Take me back before I forget how to speak."

They cleaned the area and headed back to the truck. Once their seat belts were buckled, she turned toward him. "I mean it, Wade. Thanks so much for saving me at Tim and Leah's house." Her hand shook just a bit as she raked her fingers through her hair. "I still can't believe it. Mel had so many plans before she started dating Joel."

Unsure what to say, he simply nodded as he started the truck.

"My heart hurts that I don't have the money to pay for a wedding," she continued. "I've struggled every day to make a decent life for Mel and me. My parents are missionaries in Brazil. One of my sisters is overseas in the military. Another one is a brand-new stay-at-home mom whose husband is a cop. I don't have family with unlimited resources. I can't compete."

She continued to vent the rest of the way to Tim and Leah's house. Wade listened and prayed for direction. For how to counsel Joel and Mel. And for what to do with the attraction he felt for Kristy. He parked in front of the house. Before getting out of the truck, she squeezed his hand. "Thanks to you. I can do this now."

His heartbeat quickened, and he followed her up the sidewalk. He'd need to get his dog and get out of there because he was more confused about how to handle this whole situation than he had been before the day started.

Two days later, Kristy pulled down the visor and looked at her reflection as she applied light pink lipstick. She patted her cheeks, wishing she could do something to cover the freckles that splattered across her face and gave her a more youthful appearance. She bit back a laugh. Only a teen mom who'd spent her adult life avoiding comments like "you don't look old enough to have a kid that age" would understand Kristy's need to appear more mature.

After scooping her briefcase out of the passenger's seat, she stepped out of the car and then smoothed out the wrinkles in her peach pencil skirt. As she walked toward the community college, she hoped the rhinestone she'd hot glued back on to the top of her favorite sandals stayed in place. Even though Leah and Tim were determined to pay for the wedding, Kristy planned to help foot the bill or at least help with some of the baby costs. She wouldn't have extra money for new wardrobe pieces for quite a while.

Once in her classroom, Kristy turned on the laptop and pulled up the presentation software. She took the syllabi and first-class assignments from her briefcase, and then looked over her notes.

A knock sounded at the door, and Kristy motioned for a young woman to come inside. She glanced at the clock on the wall, realizing the summer writing class would begin in fifteen minutes.

"Hi, Professor Phillips." The woman ducked her chin and waved with her free hand. The other held on to a small boy, probably three years old. The little guy's hair was a mass of red curls. His eyes were big and puffy from being awakened, and his mouth was turned down in a frown. "I'm sorry I had to bring my son. I hope it's okay."

Kristy looked back at the young woman. Her light red hair was pulled back in a haphazard ponytail. Her expression appeared just as fatigued as her son's.

"My mom couldn't watch Jonah today. Normally, it won't be a problem. I would have emailed and told you I couldn't make it…" She lifted one shoulder. "I just didn't want to miss the first class."

Kristy's heart tightened as memories washed over her: missing class when Mel had been sick, asking family and friends to watch her when schedules had changed, begging one particularly grumpy professor to allow them to simply sit in the back of the auditorium. She'd promised to leave right away if Mel had fussed. The man had stood by his no-children-in-the-classroom policy.

Kristy smiled at the young woman. "I completely understand. You'll normally have child care?"

The woman nodded. "My mom always watches him. She just had a doctor's appointment today."

Kristy pointed to the back of the room. "Why don't you just have a seat in the back beside the door? That way if he gets fussy, you can slip out without any disturbances."

"Thanks."

"What's your name?"

"Hannah Akers."

Kristy passed her a syllabus and the first assignments. "I'll go ahead and give you these in case you have to slip out."

Hannah sighed. "I appreciate it. It's not easy being a single mom and going to school."

Kristy nodded. She understood better than Hannah knew. Opening the top desk drawer, she pulled out a couple of suckers and handed them to Hannah. "These might help keep him occupied."

Hannah thanked her again and then made her way to

the back as several students entered the room. Throughout class, Kristy tried not to look at Hannah and her young son, Jonah. She tried not to remember her own struggles getting through college while caring for a toddling daughter. She tried not to allow worry for Mel and her unborn grandchild to seep through her thoughts and distract her from the lesson.

She exhaled a sigh of relief after she passed out the assignments and dismissed the class. Intellectually stimulated and emotionally overwhelmed, she contemplated going home, changing into shorts and a T-shirt and taking a walk through the White Tank Mountains.

"Professor Phillips?"

Kristy turned. One of her students, a dark-haired young man, leaned against the door frame. "Yes?"

"I'm Curt Earlywood."

He pushed away from the jamb and extended his hand. She shook it, but when he held her grip for a moment longer than necessary, Kristy pulled back. "How may I help you, Mr. Earlywood?"

"Call me Curt." He chuckled, but the sound came out more like a snort than a laugh. "My buddy took your class last semester. He said you were pretty hot."

Kristy raised her eyebrows and glared at him. "Excuse me?"

"I mean, he said you were pretty. And he said you were a really nice lady. And…" His voice cracked, and he cleared his throat and shuffled his feet. "I wondered if I could treat you to lunch."

Kristy's initial anger simmered as she realized the boy must not have intended to sound disrespectful. "Thank you for the offer, but I'll have to decline."

"How come? It's not as though we're not adults."

Kristy blinked at the immature response. With a firm

word and a narrow gaze, she would have reprimanded any other young man, but Curt seemed truly hurt by her refusal. She folded her hands together. "It would be highly inappropriate for me to go on a date with one of my students. Additionally, I'm much older than you realize."

He sneered. "I know lots of professors who go out with students."

She shook her head. "Not this one."

He released an exaggerated sigh, then shrugged. "Well, okay. It was worth a try."

She bit back a grin and nodded. "I'll see you tomorrow."

He turned to leave, then stepped back through the door. "Just out of curiosity, what are you? Like twenty-six?"

"Try adding a decade to that number."

Curt's eyes widened, and he left in a hurry. Kristy shook her head. Not only was Mel unprepared for mothering, Kristy was unable to fathom being a grandmother.

Chapter 7

Wade walked into Marley's Restaurant and Bar, one of Surprise's favorite restaurants. He'd been here before for lunch and enjoyed a turkey sandwich. The catfish dinner with fried potatoes and coleslaw had looked so delicious, he'd determined to try the meal for the church's monthly men's dinner out.

He had still been moving into his house during the previous event, so he wasn't sure what to expect. Chad Whalen, the church's music minister, had assured him Wade would have no responsibilities. Whoever wasn't busy came for the meal. They'd fellowship and eat, and then they'd go home.

Wade spied Chad in the back corner. The youth minister, Greg Rogers, stood beside him. Wade swallowed a chuckle at the visual contrast between the two men. Though only a few years apart in age, Chad looked much older than Greg. Chad's copper-colored hair was short and styled, his beard full but neatly trimmed. He wore a red polo shirt tucked into a new pair of jeans with a brown leather belt around his waist.

In contrast, Greg's black hair had been cut to look messy and even spiked out from various angles. Thick black glasses would have given him a Clark Kent appearance if not for his ultrasmall frame, which he'd covered with a hipster T-shirt and skinny jeans. When Wade had first seen Greg, he'd instantly stereotyped him to be a semi-Gothic, probable junkie. Until Wade heard him talk about Christ. Greg was sold to the Lord, 100 percent, and his unthreatening appearance and zeal for God drew in the teenagers of the community.

Wade shook Chad's hand, then Greg's. "Hey, guys. Just the three of us?"

Chad motioned to the rest area. "Freddy'll be right back."

Greg pointed to the door. "Here comes Ron."

Ron Rice, one of the older deacons of the church, grabbed Wade's hand in a death grip of a handshake. "Evening, Reverend Wade."

"Please. Just call me Wade."

Ron teased, "Take some getting used to if I call my minister just by his first name."

"Times are changing," said Greg.

Ron furrowed his brows at the younger man and humphed as he plopped down in a chair.

"How's Wilma tonight?" asked Chad. He winked, and Wade had a feeling the music minister had just averted an argument between the two men.

"She and Dortha went to dinner together, since Freddy and I are here." He looked around the restaurant. "Where is Freddy?"

"I'm here, old man." Freddy patted Ron's back. "Just

had to use the men's room." He plopped down beside his friend.

Wade glanced at the time on his smartphone. Fifteen minutes past the agreed-upon time. "Looks as if this is all of us."

Greg nodded. "A lot of people go on vacation in June."

"Usually twenty or so men show up," added Chad.

"Michael Preston was parking when I pulled up," said Ron. "Poor guy looks exhausted."

Chad wrinkled his nose. "I've heard Noah's not sleeping well." Michael walked in, and Chad motioned him to the table.

"Mel said she and Kristy kept him, and he cried most of the night," responded Greg.

"That was really nice of them to keep the baby," said Wade.

"Carrie only allowed it because Kristy's her sister," said Michael. He nodded to each of them, then sat across from Ron. "It was the best sleep ever."

Wade sat beside Michael. "I didn't know they were sisters."

"Yep. Another sister is stationed in Japan. And her parents are missionaries in Brazil. With my family living in Kentucky, Kristy is all the family we have."

The waitress arrived for their drink orders, and since each of them knew what he wanted, she wrote down their meals, as well. Wade wondered if Michael and Carrie knew about Mel's pregnancy and upcoming wedding. He imagined that while taking care of her fussy nephew, Kristy had worried about how Mel would handle the same situation. He itched to call and check up on her, but his attraction for her made him hesitant.

"Now, you know Wilma and I would watch your little guy anytime you needed us," said Ron.

"That's very kind of you," said Michael. He turned to Chad. "I meant to mention it on Sunday and forgot. That new song you presented during worship was awesome."

"It's one of my favorites, too," added Greg. "The students begged to sing it at youth group."

Freddy shifted in his seat. "It was a bit too upbeat to me."

"And too loud," added Ron. "And I'm hard of hearing."

"I don't have a problem with clapping and raising your hands at the service," said Freddy, "but there was a girl a few rows in front of us actually shaking her rear end."

Ron shook his head. "Not appropriate."

"I agree we don't want people dancing provocatively," said Chad, "but even David danced before the Lord when the Ark of the Covenant was brought back to Jerusalem."

"I bet he wasn't shaking his rear end," snorted Ron.

"I want to hold the hymnal in my hands," said Freddy. He turned to Wade. His expression implored Wade to agree. "What's wrong with the old hymns?"

"Nothing," said Greg. "But there isn't anything wrong with the contemporary songs today, either."

"It's like the different translations," said Ron. "I finally get used to the NIV, and now the reverend is reading from the ESV."

"Wade," Greg responded.

Ron narrowed his gaze at the youth minister, and Wade cleared his throat. He looked at Ron. "Yes, please call me Wade." He opened his hands. "I'm sure we can come to some compromises."

Freddy leaned back in his chair. "The older generation doesn't like all these changes, especially when they're not brought before the church for approval. And let's face it, the bulk of the financial support comes from—"

Wade lifted his hand. "I'm sorry, Freddy. I'm going

to have to stop you there." He swallowed the knot in his throat. He had no desire to upset members when he'd been pastoring the church only a month. After a quick prayer for guidance, he continued, "I never want to know who contributes what to the church's treasury. A person's giving is between him or her and God. As long as I'm pastor, I won't support a single decision that is made on the basis of appeasing those who give the most money."

Freddy lifted his eyebrows and looked at Ron. "Guess we're under new management."

"I'm not your manager," said Wade. "I'm your pastor. My job is to lead this church in following God's will. God's will only. No person."

Ron's lips parted into a slow smile. He patted Wade's hand. "That's good to hear. I think we should look into forming a committee to help us old folks—" he pointed to himself, then motioned to Greg "—and the young folks compromise in the way worship looks."

Greg nodded. "I think that sounds like a great idea."

Michael clasped his hands. "We have a business meeting tomorrow night after Wednesday-night prayer meeting. We'll bring it up then."

Wade forced a grin as the men changed the subject to baseball and the weather. A committee to help them all get along. Wonderful. He needed to add more meetings to his calendar like he needed to add more marriage-counseling sessions. But at least it was a first step.

Kristy leaned forward in the pew, rested her elbows on her knees and rubbed her temples with her fingertips. "What just happened?"

Carrie chuckled as she nudged her forearm. "You just agreed to be on the unification committee. You're going to help get all of us on the same page for worship."

Kristy sat up and glared at her sister. "Why did you nominate me for this?"

"Michael told me to." She shrugged. "And I'm glad I did. You're a terrific negotiator, mediator, debater." She flipped her wrist. "Whatever the correct term is. You were always the one to keep the peace between all us sisters."

"But I don't have time to be on a let's-make-everyone-happy team." She shook her head. "Why can't I just learn to say no?"

"Quit being such a drama queen."

Kristy glowered at her sister.

Carrie laughed outright and nudged her again. "Come on, sis. It's not so bad. You're only teaching one class this summer, and Mel won't be moving out for a couple months."

Kristy bit her tongue. She hadn't shared the big news. Noah was only two weeks old, and only a few days had passed since his digestive system had seemed to settle into his new supplemental formula. Carrie still nursed him, having adjusted to a bland diet to keep from upsetting Noah's tummy. Today was the first time Carrie had left the house, except the times she'd taken him to the doctor.

Carrie looked at her smartphone. "We need to get going. Noah's gonna want to eat in about half an hour, and I don't want Michael to give him a bottle." She glanced down at her chest. "I need some relief."

"Okay." Kristy stood. "I just need to say one quick thing to Wade."

A sly expression wrapped Carrie's face as she leaned close. "He's kinda cute, don't ya think? You've always liked dark-haired men, and those deep blue eyes of his are perfectly dreamy."

Kristy rolled her eyes. "Aren't you married? Just had a baby, even?"

"Michael really likes him. Feels like he's gonna be good for the church."

Kristy tsked. "I hope so, since we just voted him into the pulpit."

"He thinks Wade's a great all-around kind of guy. You know, down to earth and all."

Kristy nodded.

"And he's single," Carrie singsonged.

"And he's our minister," Kristy mumbled, and then made her way toward Wade before someone heard their conversation.

He looked up and smiled when she approached. Her stomach tightened as she took in the five-o'clock shadow wrapping his strong chin. Deep blue eyes drew her nearer, and she swallowed trying to remember what she wanted to ask him.

"Thanks for agreeing to serve on the committee," he said.

Standing so close to him, she noticed how broad his shoulders were. He wore a yellow polo shirt, which appeared to be just a tad small. Either that or he worked out more than any pastor she'd ever known. He picked up his Bible, and his biceps flexed with the motion.

"I think we have a good group. Very diverse," he continued. "Greg and Becca, Chad's wife, represent the younger generation. Freddy and Eustace represent the seniors."

"Guess that means we represent the middle."

"Yep."

Forcing her thoughts away from his straight white teeth and full smile, she said, "I wondered if you'd met with Mel and Joel."

"Tomorrow."

Kristy frowned. "Doesn't our committee meet tomorrow?"

He pointed to her, then himself. "We meet at seven. I meet with Mel and Joel at four."

"You must like meetings."

"They're why I became a pastor." He winked, and Kristy couldn't stop the laugh that bubbled up inside her. He studied her for a moment. "Would you like to go for a walk with me and Bo?"

"Bo?"

"My dog."

"Oh, yes. I remember him now."

"Dalmatians like attention, and they thrive on regular exercise." He tilted his head. "You could join us. We could confabulate a bit about Mel or whatever you'd like."

Kristy chuckled. "Confabulate? Really?"

"It's just a formal meaning for talk or converse."

"Oh, I know. I'm just wondering if you're studying a dictionary in your spare time."

"Only when I'm not in meetings."

Kristy enjoyed his quick wit. He surprised her each time she was around him, and her heart beat faster as she considered he might be looking up words in the dictionary just to impress or amuse her.

Carrie walked up beside them. "Hello, Wade. I'm sorry to interrupt, but we've got to go. Noah's getting fussy."

Kristy turned to Wade. "I'm sorry. I rode with Carrie, and—"

"I'll take you home," he said. "Won't be a problem."

"That would be so helpful." Carrie's eyes twinkled with mischief. "Save me a trip to the other side of town."

Kristy scowled at what she knew were her sister's matchmaking tactics. Carrie cocked her head, lifted her brows and then hefted her purse higher on her shoulder. "I'll see you later."

"You don't have to go for a walk. I can just take you home."

Kristy looked back at Wade. "It's not that."

"Your sister's just trying to set us up?"

Her face heated.

"Don't worry about it," he went on. "Someone's always trying to set me up." He puffed out his chest. "Good-looking, single pastor."

"And humble," she added.

He pressed his palm against his chest. "Of course."

"You're definitely different than any pastor I've known."

"You know I'm teasing you."

Mocking his gesture, she pressed her hand against her chest. "Of course."

He smiled, exposing the straight pearly whites that set her heart to thumping once again. "Come on. I gotta get to Bo before he chews the leg off my couch."

"He's that destructive?"

He winked. "That might be a slight hyperbole."

"I think you're trying to find a word I don't know the meaning of."

"Maybe…or catch you ending sentences with prepositions."

"You got me."

He grabbed her arm. "But I do need to get to Bo. Most likely, he needs to use the little boys' room."

Chapter 8

Wade studied the young couple sitting across from his desk. Mel's long, curly dark hair was pulled back in a ponytail. She wore a plain white T-shirt, navy blue shorts and flip-flops. A green-and-blue necklace and dangling green earrings dressed up the outfit. The glasses perched on her nose gave her a more mature appearance, but she still looked young. Too young to become a mother.

Joel's appearance wasn't much more mature. He wore long khaki shorts and a blue uniform shirt with his dad's plumbing-business logo on the front and Joel's name stitched to a badge beneath it. His blond hair was in need of a trim, and the patchy stubbles around his jaw only made him look younger.

"We've been praying together, Pastor Wade," Mel said in her high-pitched voice.

"We want to do this right." Joel's deep voice was a direct contrast. "We were both raised to wait until we were married."

"And we know the pregnancy is our fault," interrupted Mel. "We're not trying to blame anyone or anything. We've asked God to forgive us."

Joel took Mel's hand in his. "We want a love like our parents have."

Wade's gut turned. He didn't know much about Chuck and Mary, Wade's parents. Mel's dad and stepmom had been nice, but in the little time he'd spent with them, he felt pretty sure God was not the center of their marriage. And his heart broke for Kristy. While walking Bo with him, she'd shared how she'd always thought she'd marry and have a family, much like Tim and Leah, and how awkward she felt in their presence.

He opened the Bible on his desk to Ecclesiastes. "Solomon talks about the difficulty of breaking a cord with three strands."

Mel nodded. "Yes. I've heard that. A marriage is stronger when God is the third cord."

Wade shook his head from side to side. "Of course, theoretically, some want to debate if one is accurate to attribute this specific verse to marriage." He pointed. "As you can see, in the previous verses, Solomon is talking about turmoil and safety."

He glanced up at Mel and Joel, and then pinched his lips together. Now was not the time for a theoretical debate. They were here for marriage counseling. Something he was unqualified to do. Sure, on paper, he had the knowledge and background to counsel newlyweds. But as he looked at this young couple, so eager to take their mistake and allow God to mold it into something good, he realized how ill prepared he was emotionally, even spiritually, to guide them.

Leaning back in his chair, he released a long sigh. "What I mean to say is that when God is woven into your marriage, you have a better chance of withstanding life's challenges together. You love each other, right?"

Joel and Mel looked at each other and then looked back at him. They nodded, their eyes twinkling with love and adoration.

"I don't think those cords represent your love."

They frowned, and Mel started to open her mouth. Wade stopped her. "Sure, God's cord is all about love. He *is* love. Agape love, which means He's going to love both of you, no matter what."

Wade pointed from Joel to Mel. "But the two of you are human. Though you want to love each other with an unfailing love, you're still going to fail. Which is why your cords are all about commitment."

"Commitment?" Joel questioned. "I'm committed to Mel. That's why I want to marry her."

Wade sat forward and leaned against the desk. "But you have to decide now if you're going to be committed even when you don't want to be married to her."

Mel frowned. "But I hope he always wants to be married to me."

Wade glanced around his office. Books about all kinds of faith and relational topics covered two walls of shelves. He had just as many tomes loaded on his electronic reader. He didn't have personal experience as a married man, but he'd witnessed enough marriages and divorces to know that what he was trying to say was true. *How do I express it?*

He snapped his fingers. "Think of any relationship you've had, outside of the one with each other." He pointed to both of them. "Tell me someone."

"My cousin, Brock," said Joel.

"My mom," said Mel.

"Okay." Wade nodded. "Have you ever been so frustrated you didn't want anything to do with them?"

"I don't really speak to Brock anymore. We were best buds until his family moved to Michigan. Then he kinda became a jerk," said Joel.

Mel snorted. "My mom's driving me crazy right now. I avoid her every chance I get."

Wade cringed. Kristy would be devastated to hear Mel's words. "If that relationship was a marriage, you would need to fix it. No matter how you feel about the person, you're committed." He waved his hand. "I'm not talking about abuse or infidelity. Those situations have to be dealt with on an individual and different basis."

He motioned to Joel. "You'd have to work through him being a jerk." He turned to Mel. "And you'd have to deal with her driving you crazy. Does that make sense?"

He handed a packet to the couple. One of his pastor friends had emailed the papers to him earlier, and Wade had printed them for Mel and Joel. "Go through these scriptures and answer the questions together sometime this week." He picked up two sheets of paper and gave one to each of them. "But before you go, I want you both to fill out this questionnaire."

"I thought I was done with school," Joel teased.

"As long as you're alive, you'll be learning," said Wade. He stood and motioned to the door. "But I want you to answer the questions in different rooms. Bring me the papers when you're done."

"This *is* like a test." Mel chuckled.

"And we'll go over the results next week," said Wade.

Mel rolled up the paper and swatted Joel's arm with it. "You better not mess up."

Joel lifted his hands. "Just tell me the answers and I'll be fine."

Wade shook his head. "No cheating. This is a solo activity."

The couple left the office, bantering over who would get which room. Wade's heart tightened at the sight. He and Zella had done an activity much like the one he'd just given Mel and Joel. They'd worked through their individual expectations for each other, and he felt sure they'd looked at their pastor with the same love-filled, idyllic expressions.

Renewed guilt seeped through his pores. He wished he'd had the chance to prove his commitment to Zella. It was his fault he'd never had the opportunity.

He thought of the words he'd said to Mel and Joel about God's agape love. God loved them unconditionally. In his mind, Wade knew God loved him the same, and yet he couldn't seem to get past the guilt that he'd caused the accident that had taken such a ministry-filled servant from the world.

It's time to work through your guilt. His sister's words churned through his brain. But Zella's life had been worth more than two decades. He would never be able to toil hard enough to compensate for her life.

Kristy hadn't been able to get any information from Mel and Joel when they'd returned from their first counseling session. But then, her daughter had been quite perturbed with any questions Kristy had asked. After all the years of taking care of her one-and-only, Kristy thought Mel would understand she only wanted the best for her daughter. And now there was another life to consider.

She walked toward the Sunday-school room where they'd agreed to have the committee meeting. The heels of her sandals clicked against the linoleum-covered, concrete floors, and a wave of insecurity washed over her. She might have put too much effort into her appearance. She'd enjoyed talking with Wade last night, and though the idea of pursuing a relationship was something she couldn't quite wrap her mind around, she still wanted him to find her attractive.

After opening the door, she saw the rest of the unification committee sitting at a rectangular table. Eustace and Freddy sat beside one another. Freddy shook his head at something Eustace said. Greg and Becca were on the opposite side, chatting. Wade was seated between the two groups. He looked up when she walked in. He smiled, but the expression seemed forced, and she wondered if he'd had a bad meeting with Mel and Joel or if he was worried about the committee.

"We're all here," said Wade, "so let's get ready to start the meeting."

"I think we need to start with a word of prayer," said Becca. She glanced meaningfully at Freddy and Eustace.

"I was just about to suggest that," said Wade. "Becca, would you like to lead us?"

She pressed her hand against her chest, and Kristy noted her cotton candy–pink manicure with a flower design on her ring finger. Her blond curls bounced as she shook her head. "I'm not comfortable praying in public."

Wade's expression was kind. "No problem." He glanced at Kristy. "What about you?"

She wasn't overly comfortable talking with God in front of people, especially a so-obviously divided group, but the spirit nudged her heart, and she nodded and then bowed her head. Her mind whirled with all the division and disappointment she'd felt in the past two weeks. Wanting God to bring contentment and peace to her life and her church, she allowed the Holy Spirit to guide her words. "God, open our hearts to changes we would have never sought out on our own. Give us comfort with what makes us uncomfortable. May we be open…"

As she continued the prayer, God stirred her to accept the death of her dreams for Mel. As she spoke to the Lord, she heard her plans. Not Mel's. Not even God's. She had to bury what she wanted and embrace what was new and uncertain. And scary. She wanted to keep Mel tied up in a big red bow. Go to college. Become a lawyer. Get married. Start a family. No problems. No challenges. No personal choices. No room for hurt or failure.

But hurt and failure initiated growth, and growth meant change. Kristy realized afresh that her love for God had come through hurt, failure, growth and change.

After ending the prayer, she exhaled a long breath and blinked her eyes several times to keep tears from flowing down her cheeks. Wade studied her for several seconds, and she couldn't decipher his expression. Heaviness seemed to weigh in his eyes, and she wondered at the touch of pain she saw in them.

"First, we gotta talk about the music." Freddy's booming voice snapped her back to reality.

Becca frowned. "What's wrong with the music?"

Eustace leaned forward and tapped the table. "Nothing is wrong with Chad, dear. Your husband is a gifted music minister." She cleared her throat and pinched her lips together. "But a few of the songs he's trying to get us to learn are just a bit too fast for a morning worship service."

"I'm not sure God is worried about the speed of the songs." Greg stopped her. "God is looking at the heart of the worshipper."

"Of course He is," said Freddy. "But I have a hard time focusing on worship when people are dancing all over the place."

Kristy breathed a sigh of relief when Wade raised his hands. "Okay. So it sounds like one of our bigger concerns is the kind of music used during worship services."

The group nodded.

"Anything else?" asked Wade.

Becca ducked her chin and shrugged. "You preach a little longer than we're used to." She straightened. "Not that your sermons aren't terrific, but the longer services can be a challenge for the nursery workers."

"And for some of us with arthritis, who can't sit in those pews too long," added Freddy.

Kristy bit back a grin as she contemplated how Wade would react to the concern. She loved her church family, but everyone seemed to have his or her own opinion about how things should run, and most didn't seem to have compromise on their minds.

Wade jotted something down on a notepad. "Okay. Some are concerned about the length of the sermon. What else?"

"What about the Bible translation?" asked Eustace.

"I liked it better when we had baptisms at the beginning of the service instead of the end," added Becca.

"I'd like to see the youth become more actively involved," said Greg.

Freddy's voice boomed again. "That's something we can agree on, Greg. My grandson might be more willing to come to church if he saw people his own age participating."

"I bet he'd enjoy more contemporary music, as well," added Becca.

Kristy's heart twisted as the group continued to argue. This division wasn't good for the church. Everyone was seeking his or her own agenda. She offered a silent prayer for peace and then glanced at Wade. He finished writing on the notepad. Their gazes met, and she offered a slow nod to let him know she'd help him work for unity.

"Okay. I have an idea," said Wade. He held up his paper. "I've written down everyone's concerns. I'm going to make a copy for each of you. We'll meet again next week at the same time. Until then, I challenge each of you to watch, sing or read the opposite of what you prefer."

"So since I like to read the English Standard Version of the Bible, this week I'll read the King James?" asked Kristy.

Wade smiled. "Exactly."

Freddy and Becca frowned.

"I don't know," said Becca.

"Not sure I'll feel comfortable," said Freddy.

"We've all been chosen for the committee to bring unity to the church. We have to be willing to compromise." Kristy looked at Eustace and Greg. "It's just for one week."

Greg pushed his glasses higher on his nose. "I'm in."

"I suppose I'm willing to try." Eustace rubbed her hands together.

"Terrific. Let's close in prayer," said Wade.

Kristy's mind swirled as she thought of her relationship with Mel. She needed to heed her own advice. She had to talk to her daughter, but more important, she needed to listen. And compromise.

Chapter 9

Wade hooked the leash to Bo's collar. The canine obeyed the command to sit, but he panted and his tail thumped against the dirt. Wade scratched behind the overgrown puppy's ears. "Someone's looking forward to his walk."

Bo released a quick whine, then barked once. Wade patted the dog's head. "Then, let's not wait any longer."

After grabbing a water bottle and a few bags to scoop up any of Bo's natural fertilizer, Wade stood and motioned for Bo to do the same. The dog jumped to his feet, and Wade allowed him the required six feet of headway. He wished Bo's excitement over sniffing each rock and creosote bush was contagious. The week had been long and emotionally exhausting. He had a sermon ready for the next morning, but his spirit felt weary.

The Waddell Trail was a mile long. He had 1.6 kilometers each way to allow God to refresh his mind and spirit. Basking in the Lord's creation would help replenish him.

Division. He couldn't remember the last time he'd felt so restless and discontented. *God, I should be on fire. Ready to share Your good news with my new flock.*

His spirit was quiet, and he continued to follow Bo along the trail. Lonely. Another word to describe his heart. For years, he'd contented himself with working hard, heading committees, ministering to communities, leading Bible studies and prayer groups. And now, all of the sudden, he felt lonely. Maybe he'd been that way for years. So busy he was too tired to notice. But now that he'd met Kristy...

He spied a couple approaching ahead of him, holding hands. They looked to be in their midthirties. Smiling. Happy. Once they were close enough, the woman said, "What an adorable dog."

Reluctantly, Wade stopped. "Thanks."

He should want to talk to the pair. Live every moment of his life as a witness to God. And yet he just wanted to be alone. To wallow in the self-pity of division and isolation.

"May I pet him?" she asked.

"Sure." Wade forced a smile. "Bo loves all the attention he can get."

While the woman gushed over his dog, Wade and her husband talked about the pleasant weather they'd had, and he invited them to church the next morning.

After they parted ways, Wade gazed up at the clear blue sky. *God, if they do come tomorrow, I gotta be ready to preach. Lift this negativity from my heart.*

Nothing. He pushed Bo to walk faster, and the canine happily complied. His mind whirled with thoughts of Kristy and how attracted he'd become to her. At first, he'd found her pretty. But after she'd prayed over their meeting, something more had been stirred within him.

Memories of Zella washed over him more often. With them came guilt heavier and stronger than he'd felt two decades ago. The meeting with Mel and Joel had only added to his frustration. Their love, immature as it was, yanked at his heartstrings. Longing and loathing warred within him. He wanted that kind of emotion, but he didn't deserve it.

"How you doing, Pastor Wade? And what a fine animal you have there."

He blinked and turned to the woman he'd nearly barreled right past. "Wilma. I'm sorry. I was in such deep thought I didn't see you."

She clicked her tongue. "Probably pondering your sermon for tomorrow, huh?" She leaned over and petted the top of Bo's head.

He twisted his mouth. "Sort of."

Wilma rested her hand on his forearm. "I've got to tell you, your sermon about forgiveness two weeks ago really touched my heart. I've felt guilty for so long that I didn't realize I was still punishing myself."

She took a long breath, then looked back up at him. "You see, several years ago Ron had lung cancer."

"I didn't know."

"Of course you didn't. He's better now. Stage one. He had surgery, and then he was fine. Still goes for checkups every now and again."

"That's good." Wade frowned. "What does that have to do with you needing forgiveness?"

Wilma pointed to herself. "I caused it." She waved her hands. "The doctors would say that might not be the case, but in my heart, I believe I did. I smoked a pack of cigarettes a day for the first twenty years of our marriage." She shuffled her feet back and forth. "I'm fit as a fiddle, but Ron got cancer."

Wade's heartbeat sped up, and a bead of sweat trickled down his temple and cheek. A vision of Zella flashed through his mind, and he gripped Bo's leash tighter.

Wilma continued, "You read from Mark that if a man is praying and has anything against a brother, then the man needs to forgive the brother so God can forgive him." She chuckled as she clapped her hands together. "For some reason, it just hit me. I had a sister I needed to forgive. Myself." She patted Wade's arm again. "And you know what, I went home, got myself down on these old knees, and I did. I prayed to God, and I forgave myself."

She leaned over and scratched behind Bo's ears. "I'm like a new woman." She stood and lifted her fist toward the sky. "Free at last."

Wade wiped the mounting perspiration from his brow. His stomach churned, but he wrapped the older woman in a side hug. "That's great to hear."

"I'll be praying for you as you ponder the message for tomorrow. God's got great things in store for our church."

Wade watched as Wilma continued her trek down the Waddell Trail. She had a spring in her step that spoke of more than just regular exercise. Wade knew the Lord. It was no coincidence that he'd run into Wilma today and that she'd shared her experience the very afternoon he was wrestling with God over the division and loneliness he felt in his heart.

He needed to forgive himself for Zella's death. Her parents had been able to forgive him, but he'd never even tried. Didn't feel worthy. He simply didn't know how.

"When is the big day?" The petite and peppy sales associate guided Mel toward a wall of wedding gowns.

Kristy suppressed the urge to inform the woman that the *real* big day was January 13. She wanted to tell her that she'd tried to listen to her daughter's ideas about marriage, the baby and her future, but that Mel's rose-tinted glasses were going to land her in a heap of disappointment.

Instead, Kristy sneaked a peek at the price tag of one of the gowns on a mannequin. She gasped and looked at another tag. Just as bad.

"We have six weeks from today," Leah announced.

"Oh, my." The sales associate—her silver-plated badge read Jess—gasped. "We'll have to find something that either fits or needs only minor alterations that can be done here in the shop." She wrinkled her nose. "That might limit us."

"I'm not worried." Mel beamed. "We're going to find the right dress today. I can feel it."

Kristy sighed at her daughter's overenthusiastic attitude. The child was not living in reality. But then, her fiancé had practically been handed a business, and her stepmother's parents were all but giving her a house. All good things, and she didn't want Mel to have a hard start, but why wasn't Mel interested in seeking something for herself, especially after all her years excelling in school? Higher education. A trade. No matter how in love the two of them were, many marriages didn't last, and she and Joel were starting theirs under very stressful circumstances.

She sat on a padded bench in front of a dressing room, with mirrors surrounding her from every angle. Remembering the argument at their committee meeting, she determined not to fight with Mel anymore about it. She prayed when the baby came, Mel would find the desire to attend college. Her daughter was too smart not to.

"What style are we looking for?" asked Jess.

"I like the long straight gowns with thin straps and a plunging neckline," said Mel.

"No strapless?" asked Kristy.

"I'm not opposed to strapless." Mel worried the inside of her lip.

"I love pearls and lace." Leah brushed the back of her

hand against Mel's cheek. "They would look beautiful against her perfect skin tone."

Jealousy swelled within Kristy. She wanted to smack Leah's hand off her daughter's face. That skin tone came from Kristy, and from her mom before her.

"What do you think, Mom?"

Kristy's heart flipped because Mel had asked her opinion. "I saw a few dresses in the catalog that had waves or ruffles of fabric below the waistline. They were very pretty."

Mel and Leah both frowned. The sales associate rushed to Kristy's side. "I know exactly what you're talking about." She turned to Mel and Leah. "Won't hurt to try on one or two." She looked back at Kristy. "What's our price range?"

"Around seven thousand," Leah piped up.

Kristy coughed, and the petite associate's lips spread into a wide smile as she hustled off to pick out some gowns.

"That's too much," said Mel.

Leah shook her head. "My mother wants to pay for it, and that's the price she said."

Mel looked at Kristy, her eyes wide and her mouth open. Kristy shrugged and tried to look excited for her daughter. Mel still hadn't shared the news of her marriage and pregnancy with Kristy's parents or either of her aunts, but in the meantime, Leah's family had taken over the wedding.

Frustration mingled with anger within Kristy. Tim and Leah and their families had been physical and emotional bystanders in Mel's life. Kristy had been the one helping Mel study her spelling words, nursing her through childhood illnesses, comforting her when things had gone wrong.

Financially, though, Tim and Leah had always had the upper hand. The best birthday and Christmas gifts. New clothes and electronics. Now they were taking over one of the most important moments in her daughter's life. She should be the only mom helping Mel pick out her wedding gown. She shook the thought away. No. That wasn't the only problem. They were spending thousands of dollars on Mel's wedding when she shouldn't be getting married in the first place. They should be at a department store picking out dorm sheets and closet cubbies.

The sales associate returned, loaded down with dresses. "I've got a few to start with." She shooed Mel into the fitting room.

Leah sat beside Kristy. The tension between them was thick, and Kristy knew she should say something to Mel's stepmother, but she couldn't get herself to do it. Her dreams for her daughter had been shattered. Even all she'd expected, whenever she'd pictured becoming a mother of the bride several years in the future, had been taken away. Mel poured over bridal magazines with Leah. They discussed colors and flowers and arrangements like friends. In contrast, every time Kristy opened her mouth, she and Mel ended up in a fight. The fault might not lie with Leah personally, but Kristy couldn't help the jealousy that wrapped around her when the petite blonde stepmom was near.

Mel stepped out of the fitting room wearing a strapless gown with a sweetheart neckline. A thick satin sash was tied in a large bow at her right hip. Lacy waves of material cascaded from the bow to the floor. She looked amazing, and the gown would be perfect for a growing belly.

Kristy pressed her hand against her chest, and tears swelled in her eyes. "Mel, you look so beautiful."

Mel rolled her eyes. "I don't like this at all." She flipped the lace below the waistline. "I feel like Big Bird from Sesame Street."

Leah crinkled her nose. "It is a bit much. I think we should go with the original idea of a long straight gown."

Kristy nodded and blinked back tears that threatened to spill for an entirely different reason. "Let's see the next dress."

For the first time in Mel's life, Kristy was the bystander. For eighteen years, she'd placed all her hopes and dreams, every ounce of her physical and emotional being into her daughter. She'd been a fool. She could see that now. Mel wasn't able to be all Kristy wanted. She was her own person, with her own dream. Kristy had no choice but to sit back and let her daughter live her own life. And somehow Kristy would have to find hers.

Chapter 10

At Kristy's request, Wade finished grilling the hamburgers and hot dogs. Any minute, Joel and Mel and Michael, Carrie and Noah would arrive at her house for dinner. Mel planned to tell her aunt and call the rest of Kristy's family tonight. When Kristy had phoned and asked for his moral support, as her pastor, he'd felt obligated to help out.

Who was he kidding? Each passing day, he found himself more attracted to Kristy. Not just her physical beauty, but also her honest spirit and her love for her daughter and the church. Though he'd wrestled with his conversation with Wilma on Saturday, he'd made it through the sermon on Sunday and had spent a lot of one-on-one time with God on Monday. In his mind, he'd accepted God's forgiveness and forgiven himself, as well. Convincing his heart was the challenge.

Kristy stepped out onto the deck and handed him a plate to put the cooked meat on. She bit her bottom lip, her expression laced with hesitation. His protective instinct kicked in. Being near Kristy stirred his heart to accept forgiveness and move forward.

"Everything will be fine," he assured her.

She bobbed her head. "I've got potato chips, plain and barbecue, potato salad, coleslaw, a jar of pickles and plenty of condiments." She snapped her fingers. "And a fruit salad. I can't think of anything else."

He longed to wrap his arms around her and kiss the top of her forehead. Instead, he stabbed a partially charred hot dog with a fork and then set it on the plate. "Sounds delicious."

"Mom."

Mel's voice sounded from inside the house, and Kristy rushed back inside. Wade finished placing the meat on the plate and then turned off the grill and headed into the house. He set the hamburgers and hot dogs on the counter. Mel popped a grape in her mouth and waved. "Hey, Pastor Wade."

"Hello, Mel. How's the homework coming along?"

She ate a piece of pineapple. "We finished it. I can't wait until Thursday to find out what he thinks about who's doing the cooking."

"You haven't discussed the questions I made you answer before leaving last week?"

She shook her head. "Haven't really had any time. He's been working a ton. That's why he's not here tonight."

The front door opened. "Hey, sis. We're here. I don't recognize the truck..."

Carrie looked up. "Well, hey, Pastor Wade. I didn't know you'd be here tonight."

She was loaded down with a car seat in one hand and a purse and diaper bag draped over the opposite arm. "Let me help you." He took the carrier. "Kristy asked me to come, and I learned a long time ago not to turn down dinner offers. Where's Michael?"

Carrie grimaced. "Got called out on a shooting. Just me and Noah tonight."

Wade held back a groan. He was the only man at this confession/dinner party. Him and Noah. And somehow he didn't feel any male camaraderie with the three-week-old. He wished he could come up with a reason to book it out of there, but what would he say? He placed the car seat on the coffee table. He didn't have an excuse. He'd just have to endure the evening.

Kristy offered him a sheepish grin, and when Carrie and Mel picked up plates and filled them with food, she grabbed his hand, squeezed and whispered, "Thanks."

Wade's heart drummed a steady beat. He cared about Kristy. A lot. And he'd gladly hang out with her and her daughter and sister and nephew and whomever else she wanted to invite, anytime she asked. His plate filled with everything Kristy had to offer, he sat at the square table, with women facing him from every angle.

"You wanna bless our food?" asked Kristy.

Wade nodded and offered a quick prayer. Silently, he added God's blessing when the time came for Mel to share her big news.

Carrie took a bite of her plain hamburger. "I'm so glad Noah's sleeping. Car rides always put him right out, but I'll guarantee you that, since I'm trying to put food in my mouth, the little guy's gonna wake up any second."

Kristy chuckled. "That's the way Mel was."

"Guess I'll find out if my little one will be like that soon enough."

Wade swallowed a big bite of potato salad. He had assumed confession time would happen after dinner. Obviously, he was wrong.

Carrie furrowed her brows, then swatted the air. "Mel, you've got plenty of time. You'll go to college. Find you a husband—"

"I've got seven months, and Joel and I are getting married in six weeks. Actually, forty days, to be exact."

Wade took a slow drink of his sweet tea as understanding wrapped Carrie's face. Kristy tapped her fork in the coleslaw while Mel stared directly at her aunt.

"Are you pregnant?" Carrie spit out the words.

Mel lifted her chin in defiance. Wade had been impressed with her and Joel's willingness to take responsibility for their actions, and he knew their desire was to make things right with God. But Mel maintained a defiant spirit when it came to chastisement regarding the situation. And he prayed for her and Kristy that God would heal the wedge between them.

"Yes, I am." Mel crossed her arms. "And Joel and I are getting married July 27."

Carrie's jaw dropped, and she turned to Kristy. "And you're allowing this?"

Kristy grimaced, and Mel leaned closer to her aunt. "I'm almost eighteen, Aunt Carrie. I'm allowed to get married if I want."

Carrie scoffed. "Did you hear that, Kris? Guess she doesn't remember the challenges you faced." She glared back at Mel. "But then, why would she? She didn't have to be the caretaker."

"I'm sorry I was such a burden," Mel shot back.

"You were always worth it," said Kristy.

Carrie threw her napkin on the table. "You know that we love you, but that doesn't mean your mother didn't have to make sacrifices. A lot of them." Carrie's eyes widened, and her voice raised an octave. "How could you do this to your mother?"

Wade knew the discussion had the potential to get heated. One reason he'd hoped Michael and Joel would be here. As a lifelong bachelor, with only one sister whom he didn't see all that often, he had no idea what to say or if he should say anything to try to mediate the situation. Noting Kristy's anxious expression as her gaze bounced from her sister to her daughter, Wade reached across the table and placed his palm on hers. To his surprise and pleasure, she gripped his hand and held tight.

Finally! Someone with some reason. Kristy bit her tongue as Carrie and Mel argued back and forth about the upcoming wedding and pregnancy. The baby *would* be a blessing. God would take Mel and the baby's life and do immeasurable good, but life wasn't going to be easy for her daughter. And she didn't necessarily need to jump into matrimony. Grandma Phillips had always said a person should make only one life-changing decision per year. Mel couldn't take back the pregnancy, but they could pray a bit more about the nuptials.

"What is that supposed to mean?" Mel bellowed. "I haven't done anything to Mom."

Noah's cries echoed through the room. Carrie pursed her lips as she turned to undo the car seat straps. Kristy hopped up and released Wade's hand. "I'll get him. You finish eating."

She flexed her fingers. She hadn't realized she'd been holding Wade's hand, and now she missed the comfort and strength of his grip. Unbuckling her nephew, she cooed at the boy, whose face was puckering. His bottom lip quivered, and she scooped his pacifier out of the seat and popped it in his mouth, then rocked the baby side to side.

"I'm not sure I'm hungry anymore," Carrie barked. "What about school, Mel?"

Mel jutted out her chin again. "I'm not going. Going to college wasn't my dream anyway."

Carrie narrowed her gaze. "Are you kidding me? Is this some kind of joke?" She turned to Wade and shook her head. "I'm sorry you have to witness this." She pointed to Mel. "But my niece has lost her senses." She stared back at Mel. "For years, this kid has practiced her arguing skills on me. Years." She emphasized the word.

Kristy pinched back a grin. She glanced at Wade and saw his eyes danced with merriment, as well. With less than a decade between them, Carrie and Mel had grown up acting more like sisters than aunt and niece. Only Carrie could get away with ranting at Kristy's headstrong daughter like this. And maybe, when Mel settled down into bed and all was quiet, she'd think about some of the things Carrie was saying now.

"I've grown up," Mel retorted. "I have responsibilities now."

"That's right. You do. Now you get to go to school and raise a baby, just like your mama did."

"I said I wasn't going."

Carrie shook her head. "I've got half a mind to leave Noah with you more than just one night. How would you like to try a week?"

Mel jutted out her chin. "I can take care of him. Even if Mom isn't with me."

Carrie snorted. "You're right about that. You're gonna learn firsthand what it's like to be completely responsible for another human being."

Mel sucked in her breath and turned a glassy gaze toward Kristy. Her child's lower lip quivered, just as Noah's had only moments ago. She wanted to kiss away Mel's boo-boos, to make everything all right. And everything would be all right, but not without a lot of work.

"This is why I didn't want to tell her," Mel mumbled.

"What? You were gonna wait until the kid got here? I'd have found out eventually." Carrie crossed her arms in front of her chest. "Honestly, Mel. You're too smart for this."

"I can't get unpregnant, Carrie."

Kristy squirmed at the lilt in her child's voice. The mama bear within her wanted to protect her cub from the mean auntie bear.

Carrie lowered her voice. "Of course not. But you need to think about this marriage business. Are you ready for that? And school?"

Carrie took Mel's hands. Mel tried to pull away, but Carrie held tight. "I know that in your heart you want to go to school. You love to learn." She smirked. "And argue. You get it from your aunt Carrie."

Mel chuckled through her tears, and Kristy had to look away. Wade smiled at her, and she saw something she couldn't quite decipher in his gaze. Instinctively, she glanced down at her sweet nephew. His tiny fist gripped her shirt collar. He sucked his pacifier and looked up at her with big inquisitive eyes.

A new maternal urge washed over her. What would Wade's baby look like? Did he want to be a father? She relished the comfort of cuddling a newborn and dreamed of what it would be like to share the blessing of a baby with a man who loved her and the child as much as she had loved Mel.

She sucked in her breath at her wayward thinking. Her daughter was going to have a baby. She was going to be a grandmother. The last thing she needed to think about was having a baby with Wade. A man she wasn't dating. Her brand-new pastor, at that.

"I love you, Mel Bell," Carrie crooned her personal nickname for the girl.

Kristy glanced up at the ceiling and blinked several times to keep tears from streaming down her cheeks.

"I know," Mel mumbled.

"Come on. Let's go call Grandma and Grandpa and tell them. Then we'll Skype Kaitlyn in Japan." Carrie wrapped her arm around Mel's shoulder. "No one is going to be as hard on you as me."

Mel huffed. "That's for sure."

"Just promise me you'll pray about the marriage and college."

"Fine. I promise."

Kristy closed her eyes, lifting a silent prayer to God that her sister had got enough through that Mel would consider He might have a different plan. A sudden thought occurred to her. Maybe God had a different plan for the rest of Kristy's life, too. And could it possibly include a handsome single pastor?

Chapter 11

Kristy sat behind the large wooden desk at the community college, opened her laptop and logged on to the class. She clicked on the electronic Dropbox storage and checked that everyone had submitted the latest writing assignment. She frowned when she saw neither Hannah nor Curt had submitted their papers.

Curt's first assignment had been poorly done, and she wasn't overly surprised he might be late with the next one. But Hannah had done an exceptional job. Her paper had been well researched and insightful. Opening a new tab, she logged on to the class rosters. She noted that Curt was no longer listed and must have dropped the class. Not a shock. But Hannah was still there.

Kristy jotted a reminder on a Post-it note to speak with Hannah, and then she uploaded the presentation for the day. While she straightened the handouts, students filed into the classroom. She greeted them with a nod, then realized she'd forgotten to silence her smartphone.

Pulling it out of her purse, she saw a text message with only one word from Mel. Thanks. Kristy's heart swelled with gratitude. After Wade, Carrie and Noah had left, Mel had opened up about her fears concerning being a wife and mother. Despite Carrie's rebuke, Mel remained adamant in her decisions. After really listening to her daughter and praying over her own heart, Kristy wasn't sure what the best decisions were for Mel. Thankfully, Mel was open to heeding God's instruction, which meant Kristy needed to have faith and get out of the way.

"Good morning, Professor Phillips," Hannah mumbled.

Kristy took in the young woman's messy ponytail, dark bags under her eyes and disheveled clothes. "Rough morning?"

"Jonah has the chicken pox. He's been running a fever and whining and trying to scratch at the sores. I finally got him to sleep at eleven last night. By the time I posted my assignment, he was up crying again."

"You posted your assignment?" Kristy cocked her head. "For this class?"

Hannah nodded. "Yes, ma'am. It was eleven-thirty or later, but I got it in before midnight."

"Your assignment isn't showing up." She took the sticky note off her desk. "I'd even made myself a note to ask you about it."

Tears welled in Hannah's eyes as she shook her head. "I know I sent it. I've been busy and tired, but I know—"

Kristy placed her hand on Hannah's forearm. "Don't worry. Just resubmit it after class."

The young woman dug through her oversize blue-and-green tote bag. "I've got my flash drive right here. It's saved on it. I can do it right now." Her voice cracked. "I don't want you to think I'm slacking."

Hannah's fatigue was getting the best of her emotions.

Kristy understood. She'd been there a few times herself. "It's okay, Hannah. I believe you."

"I'd still feel better if I submitted it right now. Is the computer lab open?"

Kristy pinched her lips together. The lab probably wasn't open yet, especially since most of the school was on summer break. She remembered times of panic when things hadn't gone as she'd planned. "Tell you what. I'll log out of my account. You log on and turn in your assignment."

Hannah's eyes widened. "Oh, no. I couldn't do that."

"It'll make you feel better, and I insist." Kristy closed each tab on her laptop, then signed off. "Already done."

She turned the computer toward Hannah and watched as her student worked. Within minutes, Hannah had uploaded the assignment, and Kristy was again using her own account.

"You're the most understanding professor I've ever had. I try not to use being a single mom as an excuse. Try to do the best work I can and not ask for special treatment."

Kristy looked into sincere and hardworking eyes. She could have been looking into a mirror eighteen years ago. "You haven't asked for special treatment a single time yet, and your last assignment was exemplary. You have nothing to worry about. I'm familiar with the challenges you're facing."

Understanding wrapped the young woman's features. "Really?"

Kristy nodded. "And my advice to you is not to give up. You'll get there."

Hannah smiled as she hefted her tote bag higher on her shoulder, then turned and took her seat. Kristy pulled up the presentation software once again and then distributed the handouts. As her gaze passed over Hannah, she couldn't help but hope Mel would decide to take on the challenge of attending college.

Wade lifted his head and opened his eyes after leading the committee in prayer to begin their second meeting. Again, Freddy and Eustace sat on one side of the table, and Greg and Becca sat on the other. Kristy sat across from him. She looked especially beautiful tonight. Her tanned skin glowed beneath a short-sleeved, button-down white shirt. Short brown waves fanned and flipped around her face. Her blue eyes sparkled with a happiness he hoped to have the chance to ask her about after the meeting. He wondered if she and Mel had had a good conversation after the uncomfortable, unusual dinner he'd attended with her, Mel, Carrie and little Noah.

Forcing his attention to the meeting, he opened the notebook on the table. "How did everyone do with listening to different kinds of music and reading different translations of the Bible?" He tapped the table. "You know what? Let's start with one thing at a time. What did you think about different translations?"

Becca crinkled her nose. "I had a really hard time understanding the King James Version."

"I don't think the youth would relate to the King James if you read it from the pulpit," added Greg.

Freddy nodded. "I agree, Greg. I'm pretty sure my grandchildren would tune out."

"I've gotten used to the NIV anyway," said Eustace.

Wade clapped his hands. "Great. What about the New International Version and the English Standard Version?"

Eustace shrugged. "I suppose there isn't a huge difference."

"That's true." Freddy tapped the table. "But I'd want

to know what standard you were reading from, because I like to follow along."

"Fair enough," Wade said.

"I've been using the ESV with the youth for a while, so they are used to that translation," said Greg.

"I prefer ESV, too," said Becca.

Wade nodded to Kristy. "What do you think?"

She glanced from Becca and Greg to Eustace and Freddy. "We believe all of these translations are accurate representations of God's word, so I'm not sure why we're discussing it." She opened her palms. "Please don't take my comment to be combative. I just think we've hired Wade to pastor our church. He should decide on the translation he preaches."

Warmth wrapped around Wade's heart. He smiled and nodded. "Thank you, Kristy. I prefer preaching from the ESV." He turned to Freddy. "It's a great idea that I will be sure to communicate with our congregation."

"Oh, that reminds me." Becca snapped her fingers. "I meant to tell you how much I enjoyed the newsletter."

Eustace nodded. "Yes. I liked the addition of a devotional."

"And it looked great at the beginning," added Kristy with a sly smile.

"Yeah," agreed Freddy. "Kinda set the mood to read it."

Kristy lifted her eyebrows, and Wade offered a quick nod. "Thanks. Okay. Let's move on to the music."

Eustace groaned. She leaned forward, cupped her cheeks with her hands and shook her head. "I tried to listen to the contemporary stuff. The words—when I could understand them—seemed good enough, but I just don't see how playing guitars and beating drums is worshipful."

"Some of those old hymns are hardly worshipful."

Becca sat up straighter in her chair. "Chad played several for me, and I was so bored I practically fell asleep."

Greg looked at Becca. "I enjoy some of the hymns. We sang all of the old hymns in the church where I grew up." He glanced at Wade. "I usually prefer contemporary, but I still get cold chills when someone sings 'Amazing Grace' or 'Because He Lives.'"

"Humph. Back in my day 'Because He Lives' *was* a contemporary song," said Freddy. He clasped his hands. "I have to admit there were a few contemporary songs I've started to enjoy."

"Freddy," accused Eustace. "You must be joking. What would Dortha say?"

"Well, there was this one song about the oceans and having faith to keep your eyes focused on Jesus and not the waves." Freddy pursed his lips and glanced at Eustace. "The song spoke to Dortha, as well. She sang right along when she was dusting the living room."

Eustace crossed her arms. Becca cocked her head. "You gotta be willing to give things a try, Eustace."

"Now, that doesn't mean I don't like the hymns, Becca." Freddy's already deep tone sounded more like a growl. "I wasn't overly fond of most of the fast-moving music."

"Well, we could always go to two services," said Becca.

Eustace clicked her tongue. "I'd rather do that than have someone on stage, banging on drums."

"There are several churches that have done the same thing," Greg said. "One traditional and one contemporary service."

Wade lifted his hands. "Wait a minute. I don't want to talk about splitting up the church."

"Right," Kristy said. "Our committee was formed for unity." She motioned toward each of them. "That we could find a middle ground, then encourage our friends to buy in to what we've decided."

Wade's heart pounded in his chest, and he found himself caring more for her. No. His feelings were beyond caring. He was falling in love with her. She would be the perfect helpmate, a terrific encourager. Someone he could come home to and experience reason and refreshment with after a taxing, spiritually draining day.

He cleared his throat and forced his thoughts back to the meeting. "I want you all to hear something." He opened his laptop and pulled up the song he'd downloaded earlier in the day. "This song blends a traditional hymn with some contemporary sound. Let's listen, then tell me what you think."

While the song played, he studied his fellow committee members. Becca mouthed the words, and Greg silently tapped the beat with his pointer finger on the table. Freddy tilted his head. He didn't make any gestures, but his expression seemed open to the new music. Eustace, however, scowled. Wade offered a silent prayer that God would show them a common ground.

He looked at Kristy. Her chin was raised, and her eyes closed. Like Becca, she mouthed the words. Her entire person glowed with worship.

He sucked in air, trying to breathe in the devotion she seemed to feel. Many times he'd told God he'd forgiven himself, that he'd moved on after Zella's death. His heart was ready to love Kristy. His mind still battled, but he had to overcome it. He had to fight for the freedom God had given him. As soon as they closed this meeting in prayer, he was going to ask Kristy for coffee. This time not as a diversion from Mel's wedding plans, but because he wanted to spend time with her.

Chapter 12

Kristy sat in a padded maroon chair and glanced around the obstetrician's office lobby. A thirtysomething woman dressed in running shorts and an oversize T-shirt perused a magazine while rocking a car seat with her foot. A couple was seated a few chairs away from her. The woman appeared to have a month or less before her baby's due date. Several more ladies and a few men waited around the room. Kristy glanced toward the front desk, and her stomach twisted at the sight of Mel and Joel signing in for her appointment.

If their calculations were correct, Mel was eleven weeks. She blinked and swallowed the knot in her throat. Her grandchild would most likely be born before Kristy would be able to fully believe her baby was having a baby.

Mel and Joel sat down beside her. He took Mel's hand and held it in his. She leaned her head against his shoulder and then sat back up. "We should be able to hear the baby's heartbeat today."

"Mom told me the slower the heartbeat, the better chance for a boy," said Joel.

Mel nudged his arm with her shoulder. "Are you saying you want a boy?"

"Well, sure." Joel scratched his head with his free hand. "I mean, a girl would be okay, I guess, but a boy would carry on the family name."

Mel stuck her nose in the air. "A girl can keep her family name if she wants."

Joel's expression dropped, like a puppy who'd just been scolded for making a mess. "Are you saying you wanna keep your last name when we get married?"

"Of course not." Mel nudged him again. "I can't wait to become Mrs. Joel Conners."

Kristy bit her bottom lip. Did that mean Mel had renewed her decision to marry Joel? Her daughter had been more open with her, but she hadn't shared any decisions she'd made after promising Carrie she'd think through her choices. The more time Kristy spent with God, studying His word and praying for Mel and Joel and the baby, the more unsure she felt about how to advise Mel about marrying her boyfriend. *Or fiancé, I should say.*

They were young. Life would be hard. But they were both Christians. Naive. Immature. But they'd made a grown-up, outside-the-will-of-God decision to have relations before they married. They were in for a big shock when the end of January rolled around, but she had been shocked as well, when Mel had made her appearance into the world. She'd survived being a mom at eighteen. She was glad she and Tim had never married, but they'd had different life goals and had realized that early on. Contrasting ideas about God and family and what their future should look like. Joel and Mel, though young, were more in accord about what they wanted.

And yet the thought of the two of them getting married... standing before God and their families and friends and pledging to love one another until death do they part? The idea was absurd. Kristy hadn't planned on thinking about Mel's wedding for several years to come.

A red-haired woman wearing peach pants and an elephant-patterned shirt opened the door to the office. "Mel Adams."

Mel hopped out of the chair. Joel stood and grabbed her hand again. Feeling like the third wheel, Kristy followed a few steps behind them.

"How are we doing today?" asked the nurse.

"Great," Mel bubbled.

She pointed to a scale. "Go ahead and step on there."

Mel passed Joel her purse while Kristy tried to make herself small by pressing as close to the wall as possible. The nurse checked Mel's temperature and blood pressure, then the three of them followed her to a room. Mel sat on the bed, and Joel squeezed between the bed and the wall. Kristy sat in a chair, again feeling very out of place.

"Are you having any symptoms you're concerned about?" The nurse flipped her hand. "Throwing up too much? Excessive cramping?"

Mel shook her head. "I feel pretty good. Just a little nausea." She placed one hand on her stomach. "I go to the bathroom. Like, a lot." Her face reddened, and she glanced at Joel, then turned away quickly.

"That's perfectly normal." The nurse flipped a paper over. "Your chart says you should be about eleven weeks. We should be able to hear the baby's heartbeat today."

"That's why we're all here," Joel piped up. His face shone with pride as he pushed a strand of hair behind Mel's ear.

The gesture was so natural and sweet, Kristy felt as

though a fist clenched her heart. It was obvious Joel loved Mel. Would that love last forever? Was he mature enough to make a commitment to her and keep it? She thought of all the coworkers, even fellow church members, who'd got divorces. Some had married young, but some hadn't. What was the key to staying married?

She knew what her parents would say. *You stay together and work it out.* Just thinking about it, she could almost hear her mother's voice when Carrie and Michael had got engaged. *You won't like him every day of your marriage, but you stick it out with him until you do like him again. And don't worry, you will.* A grin split her lips at the memory.

The door opened, and the doctor walked in. He extended his hand. "How are we doing, Mel?"

"Anxious to hear the baby's heartbeat," she responded.

He shook Joel's hand, then Kristy's. "I bet you are."

Turning away from them, he washed his hands, then put on latex gloves. He picked up the Doppler machine and then instructed Mel to lie back on the table. After applying gel, he placed the Doppler monitor on her belly.

Mel released a slight gasp, and Kristy placed her hand over her mouth. She felt as though she were in someone else's body. *Her* daughter wasn't lying on a table with a monitor on her abdomen. *Her* daughter was going to college. *Her* daughter was going to make perfect grades. Become an amazing lawyer.

Then a rhythmic beat filled the room.

"Found it," said the doctor.

Tears streamed down Mel's temples, and using tender motions, Joel brushed them away. Kristy felt her own heart beat faster as the doctor turned up the monitor and the sound grew stronger. That was her grandbaby.

* * *

Wade motioned for Mel and Joel to have a seat on the couch in his living room. "Thanks for being willing to switch locations. The church's air-conditioning should be fixed tomorrow."

"Mom said the committee meeting was postponed for tonight." Mel sat down and crossed one leg over the other. She seemed more at peace than the previous time he'd seen her, which had been when she and Carrie had battled about Mel's choices for the future. Joel sat beside her and took her hand in his. Every time Wade saw the two of them, Joel was reaching for her hand.

Bo scratched at the back door, then whined a wounded plea. The overgrown pup knew Wade had guests, and he'd probably cause a ruckus the entire counseling session.

"I forgot you had a dog," Joel said.

"He's such a cutie. Let him in, Pastor Wade." Mel jutted her thumb toward Joel, then herself. "We don't care if he jumps on us."

"I don't want him to be a distraction."

"Don't worry," said Mel. "We'll focus."

"Yeah. I'll just pet him and listen at the same time," added Joel.

The two sounded like young teens begging their dad to let them see the new puppy in the house, and yet in a month's time, they'd be newly married. They'd be parents in January. They'd grow up with their son or daughter, but they could still be good parents if they kept their focus on God's will for their and the baby's lives.

Wade let Bo in the back door. The dalmatian's tail wagged as he dashed into the living room to sniff out the guests. "Sit, Bo," Wade instructed.

The canine plopped down beside Joel. "What a great

dog!" Joel petted his head, and Bo offered his paw. After shaking, Joel laughed. "He's smart, too."

Wade clapped his hands as he took the chair across from the couple. "How have you been the past couple weeks?"

"Great," said Joel.

Mel added, "We finished the reading and questions you gave us, based on 1 Corinthians 13."

"What did you think?"

Mel's eyes twinkled with delight. "It was really cool to read the Bible and pray together. We've never done that before."

"I liked the part where we talked about keeping no records of wrongs." Joel elbowed Mel. "She's not supposed to badger me about my mistakes."

"And he'll have to be patient when I *accidentally* spend too much at the mall."

Wade furrowed his brows. "Let's not focus on what you shouldn't do but rather on what love means. You're human. You won't be perfect, but you can strive to love and think of the other first."

"We're just teasing, Pastor Wade. Actually, this weekend I had the opportunity to show love through patience," said Mel.

"She did." Joel nodded. "We'd planned a date last Friday. She'd got all fixed up, but one of our customers had a plumbing emergency. None of the other guys were able to take the job on short notice."

"So he went, and I stayed home with a movie rental and a bag of microwave popcorn."

"And she wasn't mad," said Joel.

Mel shook her head. "I really wasn't. I knew it wasn't his fault."

Wade smiled and nodded his head. "That's a great

example. There will be many times in your marriage when plans will go wrong or one of you will let the other one down. You have to stay committed despite the challenges."

He picked up the folder off the coffee table and pulled out the two questionnaires they'd filled out two weeks ago. "Have you discussed your answers?"

Joel shook his head. "We waited. Just like you suggested."

"I tried to get him to talk." Mel twisted her mouth and rolled her eyes. "But the guy was like a steel trap."

Wade chuckled. "Okay. You both answered some basic questions about your preconceived ideas about your roles after marriage. Who does the laundry, the cooking, pays the bills and whatnot." He handed the papers back to them. "Read over your fiancé's responses. Do you have like-minded expectations?"

Wade patted his leg, and Bo sat beside him while the couple looked at each other's answers. Mel hadn't mentioned anything about if she'd considered Carrie's suggestion to wait a while to have the wedding. He wondered if Mel had even told Joel about the confrontation she'd had with her aunt. He glanced up at the clock on the wall. Kristy had agreed to meet him for dinner after the session. Though he conceded to the possibility that she might try to pry information out of him, he hoped she genuinely wanted to spend time with him, as well.

"You expect me to do all the laundry?" Mel's question interrupted his thoughts.

Joel shrugged. "My mom always has. I just figured that's the way it would be."

"I'm fine with doing it, but I want you to take care of cleaning the toilets." She wrinkled her nose. "They truly make me want to barf."

"I don't have a problem with that. I spend a good part of my day looking at toilets. What's one or two more?"

Wade rubbed his hands together. "This is great. You're doing exactly what this activity is meant to do—look at what the other expects and then compromise on the expectations."

Mel flipped the paper over. "Looks like we thought the same things about most of these questions."

Wade affirmed her remark. "Actually, I was surprised at how well you seemed to know each other."

"We've dated two years," Joel commented.

"True, but most teenagers don't seem to understand each other that well."

"That's why we're going to make it." Mel stomped her foot and added a single, definitive nod of her head. "Joel and I talked about my—" she cleared her throat "—discussion with my aunt Carrie. We're not going to put off the wedding."

Wade didn't comment. Besides their ages, he didn't have any real objections. They wanted to follow the Lord, and they were already going to have a child together. He wondered if she'd shared the decision with Kristy.

"Did you see the last line?" Joel pointed to the paper in Mel's hand. "I want to get married, but I agree with Carrie on one thing."

"You want me to go to school?"

Joel raked his fingers through the mop of hair on his head. "You're too smart, Mel. You have too much potential. I want you to start school this fall. Just take off spring semester when you have the baby."

Tears welled in Mel's eyes. "You think we can do it? I want to. But I didn't want to put extra pressure on you."

"Of course we can. I'll be more stressed if my brilliant wife doesn't go to college."

Wade scratched behind Bo's ear and chewed the inside of his lip as the young woman wrapped her arms around Joel's neck. They were young, but they understood what love was. With God's guidance, they would be just fine.

Chapter 13

Kristy pressed her back against the wall that had a green bull's-eye in the center and various angular red fluorescent shapes around the corners. She looked down at the flashing purple vest adorning her upper body and the laser gun, which glowed the same bright purple each time she pressed the trigger. How had she been talked into this?

A brown-haired boy who couldn't have been older than nine spied her again and started shooting his red rays at her. She jumped and ran around the walls in search of another hiding place. Aliens with oversize heads and bulging eyes stared down at her in the Area 51–themed arena.

Tilting her head, she wished she could hear someone drawing near her. From this angle, she felt sure she could do some laser-tag damage. Especially to the nine-year-old. Or Wade. She still wasn't sure what he'd said to get her to agree to this.

The boy jumped out from behind a wall to her right.

Another person hopped out from the left. The two blasted her at the same time until she lifted her hands in the air. "I've never been a fighter," she squealed.

The game ended, and she saw that her second attacker was Wade. He laughed. "I don't know if I agree with that statement. You've got a lot of spunk."

They turned in their equipment. The group of children who'd been stuck with her on their team scowled when she passed by them. She shrugged and motioned to Wade. "I knew I'd be awful. He made me do it."

Though Wade laughed, the children's expressions didn't change. He pulled a few bills out of his jeans' pocket. "Here. Play another couple games. I'm not surprised she was awful. I take full responsibility for your loss."

The kids cheered, and Wade leaned back in a full belly laugh.

Kristy narrowed her gaze and punched his arm. "Hey! This was all your idea. I've never been in a laser-tag arena, much less participated in one."

He continued to goad her. "You should have seen yourself. Hiding in all the corners."

She pointed to the Cosmic Golf game. Unlike any course she'd ever seen, this one was played in the dark. The course, clubs and balls were lit up with fluorescent lights. This was her first time to Wazee's World. The place was terrific for kids. In addition to the laser tag and miniature golf, there were inflatables and a snack bar. "We gonna play?"

Wade lifted his right shoulder. "If you want."

Kristy clapped her hands and then rubbed them together. She might not have played at this miniature golf course before, but she'd mastered others. "Let's see who'll be the big loser now."

He clicked his tongue and winked. "You're on."

The course was only nine holes, half the length of a regular one. Adjusting to aiming at lit-up holes was a bit trickier than Kristy had originally thought. The first hole, she putted twice, and Wade made it in one.

"Oh, Kristy, Kristy." He shook his head and puckered his lips in feigned pity. "I should have told you my nickname before we started."

"What's that?"

"Winning Wade." He made a muscle and twisted his fist left to right. "I can't even remember the last time I lost."

"Well, Mr. Humility. Mark my words. Tonight is the night."

With determination, Kristy analyzed the second hole. She mentally calculated the best angles and the amount of strength to put behind the swing. This time she made a hole in one. She gave Wade two thumbs-up. "It's on."

They continued to banter as they made their way through the holes. Kristy busted out laughing when Wade snorted after he missed an easy putt. Her gut ached from the muscle strain, and she realized she couldn't remember the last time she'd had so much fun.

The game ended in a tie. Wade offered his hand. "Truce?"

Debating if she wanted to challenge him to another round or accept his gesture, she tapped her finger against her cheek. Wade stuck out his lower lip and blinked several times. She chuckled and accepted his hand. "Truce."

Before she had time to respond, he pulled her close and wrapped his other arm around her. His warm breath tickled her ear as he whispered, "I still beat you at laser tag."

A chill rushed down her spine. He must have realized their closeness, because the blue of his eyes seemed to darken with the intensity of his gaze. He looked down at her lips, and she sucked in her breath. What would she do if he kissed her? She wanted him to kiss her. Wanted it so much she leaned forward.

Wade jumped back and scratched his stubbly jaw. "What do you say we go get something to eat?"

Kristy's heart plunged. She couldn't tell if he was nervous or if he really didn't want to kiss her. He was the pastor of the church. She shouldn't want him to anyway. "That sounds good."

They headed to the snack bar and ordered slices of pizza and soft drinks. Sliding into the booth, Kristy decided not to worry whether or not he wanted to kiss her. He was her pastor, new to the community, hadn't made a lot of friends, had a lot to deal with at church… Just a plethora of adjustments. He'd become a good friend. She didn't want to think about romantic interests anyway. Her daughter was getting married and having a baby. She was about to be a grandmother. The last thing she needed was a boyfriend.

Kristy picked up her slice and blew on it for several seconds. She had such a good time with Wade. He was easy to talk to. He truly cared about things, including her daughter and the church, specifically. When she felt overwhelmed, he seemed to sense it.

She kind of hoped he wanted to kiss her.

When the church service ended, Wade asked one of the deacons, Ron Rice, to close in prayer. Wade made his way to the front door so he could shake hands with the parishioners as they left. He pulled a mint out of his pocket, took off the wrapper and then popped it in his mouth. The piano came alive, and he straightened his posture and smiled.

"Wonderful message, Pastor," said a woman. She took his hand and patted the top a couple of times before releasing him. Her husband nodded as they moved out the door.

"Hey, Pastor Wade." One of the preteen boys skittered

past him and then ran to the play area at the side of the church.

"Be careful," Wade called when two more boys raced past him to follow the first.

Holding her five-year-old daughter's hand, Becca shook Wade's with her free one. "I've noticed the sermons have been a bit shorter."

"Has that helped the nursery workers?"

She nodded. "It really has." She released his handshake and brushed a stray hair away from her cheek. "I didn't mean you shouldn't preach what God calls you to—"

Wade stopped her. "I understood completely. I have no intention of hindering the Holy Spirit, but I don't want to wear out our volunteers, either."

"I'm glad you understand what I meant."

Her young daughter tugged Becca's hand as she grabbed the front of her dress. "Mom, I gotta go to the bathroom."

Wade tapped the little girl's nose, then pointed to the restroom and looked at Becca. "You better listen to this cutie."

While they scurried down the hall, he saw Michael and Carrie approaching him. He lifted his arms, palms up. "Where's that sweet baby?"

"He's here." Michael took his hand in a firm shake.

Carrie motioned around the corner. "He started to fuss during the service, so Kristy took him to the nursery for us."

"Which was very nice, because we haven't been able to attend an actual church service in over a month," added Michael.

A vision of Kristy holding baby Noah to her chest traipsed through his mind. She was such a naturally beautiful woman, and she loved so completely. And at only thirty-six, she wasn't too old to have another child. *One who shared his last name.*

He blinked several times to push the thoughts away. He was thankful Michael and Carrie couldn't read his mind.

He glanced at Carrie and noted her sly grin. He furrowed his brows. At least, he was pretty sure they couldn't read his thoughts.

Carrie tilted her head. "Kristy mentioned the two of you went to Wazee's World yesterday."

Michael's jaw dropped. "You did? I've been wanting to check out that place. The owners are big military supporters. You know I'm still in the National Guard."

Wade hoped Michael would keep talking about the military so that Carrie didn't ask any more questions. By the mischievous expression on her face, Wade felt sure she planned to say more.

Carrie wrapped her arm around Michael's elbow. "She called last night. Said she had a terrific time. That you'd even tied her at miniature golf."

Michael's eyes widened. "Wish I'd been there. I'd have loved to see Kristy lose."

"Tie," said Carrie.

Wade winked. "I went easy on her."

Carrie blew out her breath. "I doubt it. I think she was just distracted."

Michael wrinkled his nose. "Yeah, I heard the course has all black lights. That could throw a person off."

"Or a person could be distracted by the company," said Carrie. "Especially if she kinda likes him."

Wade swallowed the almost-melted mint. It scratched his throat going down, and he coughed twice. He searched his brain for a proper response or a way to change the subject. He liked Kristy. A lot. He'd prayed for a good hour last night, begging God to help him focus on his sermon and not their near kiss.

"Did she tell you about their parents?" asked Michael.

Carrie elbowed him in the side. "We just found out late last night."

Wade offered a silent prayer of thanks that Michael had not caught on to Carrie's goading. "What about them?"

"They'll be able to come for the wedding," said Michael.

Carrie added, "They've been trying to take a furlough from Brazil so they could meet Noah. It was looking like August, but when they found out about Mel, too, Dad just called a few people and made the trip happen a little bit earlier."

"I know Kristy and Mel will be so happy to have them here. If Kaitlyn could come—"

Carrie interrupted Wade. "The military isn't quite as easy. We are trying to figure a way that maybe we can Skype her during the wedding ceremony—"

"Wedding ceremony?" Eustace's voice sounded from a few feet away. She touched Carrie's arm. "Just who is getting married, dear?"

Carrie's face reddened. Wade inwardly battled if he should just come out and tell Eustace. Kristy planned to place invitations on the welcome table the next Sunday, but so far, they hadn't made a public announcement about the wedding. Or the pregnancy.

Michael drew his wife closer to his side in a protective motion. "Well, Joel and Mel have decided to get married." He jutted his chin. "Kristy is giving out invitations next week."

"Well, now." Eustace's face contorted into a less than Christian-like smile. She glanced behind her. "Did you hear that, Ida? Mel and Joel are getting married."

Wade's heart twisted. He needed to pray for this woman more. Something in her enjoyed negativity, confrontation and gossip.

"Oh." Ida covered her mouth with her palm. "That Mel is such a beautiful girl. She'll make a lovely bride."

Wade exhaled as Carrie relaxed her shoulders. "Thank you, Ida."

Eustace narrowed her gaze. "I heard there might be a reason the two are getting married so quickly."

Anger twisted in Wade's gut. Carrie opened her mouth, but Wade blurted out, "Eustace, I think that's something you should ask Kristy or Mel. Or better yet, simply attend the wedding and be happy for the young couple."

"Well." Eustace puffed out her chest and pinched her lips together in an angry line.

Ida released a nervous laugh as she guided Eustace out the door. Wade rubbed his hands together and prayed God would temper his raging emotions. Michael and Carrie smiled, but they headed down the hall to the nursery. After a few more goodbyes from church members, Wade was able to calm his racing heart. The last time he'd felt so protective of a woman had been when he'd fallen in love with Zella. He'd sworn never to feel that way again, but his heart exposed the truth. He loved Kristy.

Chapter 14

Kristy said goodbye to Carrie, clicked her phone off, then plugged it into the charger. She fluffed the pillows and sat them up against the headboard of her bed. Grabbing a devotional magazine off the nightstand, she slid under the covers and turned to the correct date. She read the first paragraph and realized she had no idea what the author had said. She read the paragraph again and then closed the magazine in frustration.

She stared up at the ceiling, anger swelling within her at what her sister had just relayed. Eustace was such a busybody. She savored the latest gossip, then relished her disdain for whomever she deemed sinful. Shifting on the bed, she punched the pillow behind her to plump it up better. She covered her face with her hands before raking her fingers through her hair.

I didn't want this for Mel. She gripped her hair at the base of her neck. Her mind replayed the looks cast in her direction from eighteen years ago. Pity. Anger. Disgust. Disappointment. One face after another flitted through her brain. Mel had graduated. At least she had that. She wouldn't be a kid in high school sitting in metal desks lined in a row and raising her hand for permission to use the restroom...

She made a fist and pressed it against her lips. *God, hearing the baby's heartbeat was amazing. My precious grandchild.* A tear slipped down her cheek. *But I didn't want Mel to experience what I did. The judgment of so many. People can be so...*

"Mom!"

Mel's frantic scream interrupted the prayer, and Kristy jumped out of the bed.

"Mom!" Mel screeched again.

Kristy ran down the hall and into the bathroom. "What is it?"

Mel's hands shook, and her chest heaved with sobs. "I'm bleeding!" She grabbed the front of Kristy's nightgown. "Momma, what's happening?"

Kristy grabbed a sanitary napkin from under the sink and handed it to Mel. "Get ready. We're going to the hospital."

Mel wrapped her arms around Kristy. "I'm so scared, Momma. I don't want to lose the baby. Help me, Momma." Her voice caught as another sob slipped through her lips.

Kristy swallowed back tears at the desperation in her daughter's voice. She already loved the grandchild growing in her daughter's womb. Hearing the baby's strong and constant heartbeat had stirred her maternal instinct. She cupped Mel's cheeks with her hands, kissed her forehead and then whispered, "God, please protect our baby."

Without letting go of her cheeks, she looked into her

daughter's eyes. "Calm down. Get ready. We're going to the hospital. Okay?"

Mel swallowed hard and nodded, then rushed to her bedroom. Kristy threw on a T-shirt and shorts and then slipped on her flip-flops. After grabbing a couple of towels, she picked up her purse and keys off the counter, and within minutes, they were heading to a doctor. Mel's phone beeped every few seconds, and Kristy realized she had texted Joel.

"Is he meeting us there?" she asked.

Mel nodded, then a cry sounded from her lips. "I'm so scared."

"God, calm Mel's nerves," Kristy prayed as she swerved right onto the next road. "Give the doctor wisdom—" she flipped the blinker, and then turned right again "—to know what is causing the bleeding." She slowed down as she turned in at the hospital's emergency driveway. "Please keep our baby safe."

They hustled into the emergency room. The place was practically empty. *Thank You, Lord.* Kristy signed in and gave the clerk their insurance information. Within minutes, a nurse took them back to a makeshift room with cubicle curtains for walls. Mel was so upset that the nurse helped change her into an open-back robe and then got her situated to see the doctor.

The nurse left and then returned a moment later and assisted Mel into the wheelchair. "We're gonna move to an ultrasound room. Okay?"

Kristy and Mel nodded and the nurse wheeled Mel out with Kristy following close behind. Within minutes, a gray-haired woman walked into the room. "I'm Dr. Stower. I'm going to go ahead and do the ultrasound myself, all right?"

Fresh tears streamed down Mel's face, and her bottom

lip quivered. Kristy tried to choke back her fear, but she didn't know how much longer she could last. Dr. Stower patted Mel's leg. "Settle down, sweetie. Sometimes things are perfectly fine."

Sometimes. The doctor's word replayed in Kristy's mind like a broken record. Joel arrived just as Dr. Stower began the ultrasound. The screen came to life with shapes, and Kristy peered at it, trying to decipher each part of her grandchild.

The woman moved the instrument, then pointed to the small beating shape. "Strong heartbeat right there."

Mel burst into tears, and Kristy swiped away a few of her own with the backs of her hands. Joel kissed Mel's palm. "The baby's okay, right?"

The doctor moved the instrument again, this time showing them the baby's profile. His or her head. Arms. Legs. Hands. Feet. The baby was perfect.

"I'm going to keep looking, but everything looks great so far."

She measured the baby's head from various angles. "Are you about twelve weeks?"

"Yes," Mel whimpered. "I'm twelve weeks tomorrow."

Joel pointed to the clock on the wall. "It's after midnight. Actually we're twelve weeks today."

Kristy's heart warmed at his words. *We're.* He had no intention of leaving Mel alone through the pregnancy and childrearing. His loyalty to her daughter was something she appreciated and hoped didn't disappear as life got more difficult.

The woman pushed a couple of buttons, and photos of the ultrasound streamed out of the bottom of the machine. She pulled off her plastic gloves. "You'll need to call your doctor in the morning, but my guess is you've had some breakthrough bleeding."

"What's that?" asked Kristy.

She looked at each of them, then focused on Mel. "If you weren't pregnant, it would be time for your menstrual cycle. Sometimes women will experience some bleeding at that time. Did you spot at all at eight weeks?"

"No." Mel's lip trembled as she shook her head.

"That's okay." The lady patted her leg. "It's still possible to have some bleeding now. I suggest you call your doctor in the morning and set up an appointment. Stay in a resting position, lying on your left side, until your doctor's able to see you. Okay?"

Mel and Joel nodded at the same time. Mel got dressed, then looked at Kristy. "Mom, I'm going to ride back to the house with Joel."

Kristy opened her mouth, then shut it. She wanted to take care of Mel, her baby.

Then Kristy nodded. Mel wasn't her baby anymore.

When he received Joel's text, Wade hopped out of bed and threw on some clothes. Bo barked and wagged his tail, but Wade petted his head and said, "You can't go this time, boy. I'll be back soon."

His phone beeped again. He pulled over and parked in front of a house. The text read they'd left the hospital and were headed back to Kristy's. The baby appeared to be fine. Wade bit his bottom lip, unsure what to do. Should he go home and wait until morning or head over there and offer his help in any way they needed him tonight?

His desire to protect Kristy won out, and he turned his truck toward her house. When he pulled into the driveway, Kristy was getting out of her car. Joel's truck was already parked and empty. He and Mel must have got there before her. He waved and walked up beside her. "She's okay?"

Kristy nodded. "They think so."

"Joel said the baby's okay, too."

"Seems to be." She opened the front door, and he walked inside. Joel sat on the couch with his elbows propped on his knees and his head in his hands. "Where's Mel?" asked Kristy.

He looked up, and Wade saw the boy's eyes were puffy from crying. He blinked several times as he motioned to the hall. "Putting on some pajamas."

Kristy nodded, then looked up at him.

"I won't stay." He opened his hands. "I just wanted to let you all know that I'm here if you need anything at all."

"Pastor Wade." Wrapped in an oversize red robe Mel walked into the living room. Joel jumped off the couch, then fluffed a pillow and made her lie down. "Will you pray for our baby?"

"Absolutely."

They joined hands, and Wade asked for God's protection on them and for His mercy that the little boy or girl would be healthy and safe. When he ended the prayer, he wiped a tear from his eye. He'd come to love this family so much.

"Kristy, may I stay here?" Joel's voice was low. "I can't stand to think something could happen, and I wouldn't be here."

Kristy frowned and shook her head.

"Please," Joel pleaded. "I'll sleep on the couch."

"Please, Mom. I'll feel better if Joel is here," said Mel.

Kristy continued to shake her head. Wade knew she didn't want to be the bad guy, but even after all that had happened, she didn't feel comfortable having her daughter's fiancé sleep in her home. He wasn't sure he knew what he would say if he were in the same situation. "Tell you what. I'll stay, too."

He cringed as soon as the words left his lips. What was

he thinking? He looked around the living room. Where would he sleep? The recliner?

"What?" the three of them asked in unison.

He cleared his throat. "Sure." He pointed to the chair. "I'll just sleep on the recliner. You know, stay in here with Joel. It won't be like you're having your daughter's fiancé overnight. You'll be having the pastor, too."

A chuckle slipped from Kristy's and Mel's lips, and Joel laughed outright. "It might not look too good for you, the pastor, to be spending the night with two single women, either."

He grinned. "But I'll do it just the same."

Kristy swatted the air and released an exaggerated breath. "Fine. You both can stay and sleep on the couch and recliner." She took blankets out of the hall closet. "But you're both going to have sore backs and necks in the morning."

She helped her daughter to her feet and guided her to the bedroom. Kristy waved as she walked down the hall. "Sleep tight, boys."

Wade and Joel settled into their sleeping places. Wade pulled a blanket over his body and then leaned the recliner back as far as it would go.

"Thanks for offering to stay, Pastor Wade." Joel's words came out as half yawn. "She'd have never let me be here if you hadn't volunteered."

"No problem," he answered. "I understand young love." He thought of Zella. She had been so full of life. He'd have done anything for her. Thinking again of Wilma's words of finally forgiving herself, he basked in God's unexplainable ability to love him no matter what he'd done. Zella would have never wanted him to live as he had the past two decades, always striving for the unattainable—to work harder, be better, do more and never forgive himself. And she would have loved Kristy.

As Joel drifted off to sleep, Wade lay awake thinking of his newfound love for Kristy and contemplating what he should do. How he should tell her. *If* he should tell her.

A soft shuffle sounded against the floor. He looked up and saw Kristy in a large robe, heading to the kitchen. The back door opened, and he heard a chair move across the wooden deck. Not wanting her to know he was still awake, he feigned sleep until he heard a muffled cry.

He sat up and listened more closely. The whimper sounded again, and Wade slipped out of the chair. He wasn't sure she'd want his company, but he couldn't bear for her to be upset and him not help in some way.

He opened the door all the way, and Kristy gasped and hopped up. Recognition lit her eyes, and in one quick motion, she wrapped her arms around him and buried her face against his chest. Wade's heart twisted as he held her tighter and rubbed her back.

"I was so scared," she cried into his chest. "I already love that baby."

He continued to hold her, relished the thought that he might be able to make her feel better or safer in the slightest of ways. After too short a time, she pulled away from him and wiped her eyes with her hands. "I'm sorry. I've blubbered all over you."

He looked down at his wet shirt, then gazed back at her. "Anytime."

She sniffed, then moved past him, back into the house. "We better get to bed. It's going to be daylight before long."

Wade sat back in the recliner and covered himself once again with the blanket. He wouldn't sleep a wink tonight, and it would have nothing to do with the discomfort of the chair.

Chapter 15

"Is this close enough?" Kristy grimaced as she held up her latest attempt at an invitation. She'd taped a small photo of Joel and Mel to fuchsia card stock. Lacing pink-and-purple polka-dot ribbon through holes at the top, she'd attached the paper to the top of a larger piece of purple card stock, which contained the actual information about the wedding.

"Mom," Mel whined. She reached over from her chaise longue and took the invitation. "The holes don't match. You've got to punch both papers at the same time. See how the words are showing." Mel touched the bright violet page. "The photo and pink paper are big enough to cover the information on the purple paper if you position the holes right."

Leah pointed to Kristy's three other failed attempts at putting the homemade invitation together. "But look how much better you're doing. The next one will be perfect."

Her condescending tone grated on Kristy's nerves, and

she pushed away from Mel's father and stepmother's dining room table. "I think I need to use the ladies' room."

Leah motioned down the hall. "Third door on your left. You may have been there before, but we just redid it recently and moved a few things around."

Noting the pile of thirty or more perfectly completed invitations in front of Leah, Kristy scowled as she walked down the hall and into the bathroom.

She hadn't wanted to make invitations in the first place. She was all thumbs when it came to crafting. And yet she had to admit it had given Mel something to do while she heeded the doctor's orders and lounged for a few days. Her obstetrician agreed with the ER doctor's diagnosis of breakthrough bleeding. For two days, Mel had remained on her left side, but she wasn't one for sitting still, and the invitations were keeping her hands busy.

Kristy turned on the light and mumbled, "You've got to be kidding me."

The half bathroom was as big as her master bath. White chair railing split the walls in half. Both top and bottom were painted a faux-marble style using tan and gold colors. The dark tile floor matched the circular mirror with ornate trim, and the brown bowl sink sat on top of a mahogany table. Orchids and three pillar candles decorated each side of the basin. A large gold-framed picture of a yellow floral design hung above the toilet. She glanced down at the baseboard. Even the baseboards were stately.

Kristy brushed her finger across the top of the picture frame and then curled her lip. Not even a speck of dirt. She looked at her reflection in the mirror, noting the stress blemish that had formed on her chin. "I hate her," she whispered. "God, I know I'm not supposed to hate people. I'm supposed to love and pray for my enemies…"

She closed her eyes. "But I really, truly, one hundred percent can't stand her."

She washed her hands using deliciously scented lemon soap, then dried them on the soft, fluffy gold-trimmed hand towel, which boasted a large gold *A*. "She has everything I wanted."

Adding guilt for her mean thoughts to her already wounded ego, she headed back to the dining room.

"Leah and I came up with an idea," said Mel.

Leah passed Kristy a stack of envelopes and a notebook. "You write down addresses while we finish invitations."

Kristy nodded. She liked that idea much better than trying to figure out how to line up those two pieces of paper and punch the holes just right.

"Mom, I haven't talked with you much since our last counseling sessions," said Mel.

"How are those going?" asked Leah. She leaned forward and placed her hand on Mel's arm. "I know the pastor requires them, but are you finding them helpful?"

Kristy bit her tongue. Of course a little counseling would be helpful. She and Joel were practically babies themselves.

"We really like it," said Mel. She grinned at her mom. "I guess you figured out I don't want to postpone the wedding like Aunt Carrie suggested."

"Postpone?" Leah furrowed her brows. "Goodness, no. We already have a caterer. We've ordered the cakes."

Mel's expression begged Kristy not to respond. With great effort, Kristy pinched her lips together and gripped the pen tighter in her hand.

"We're not postponing, Leah. Joel and I are still getting married in twenty-four days."

Kristy pressed the calendar on her smartphone. Was

the date really that soon? It didn't seem possible, but Mel was right. Only three and a half weeks.

Mel lifted her finger. "There is one change of plans I think you'll be happy about, Mom."

"We can't change the date." Leah shuffled in her seat like a chicken that had got her feathers ruffled. "We're working on invitations as we speak."

"I promise the date is the same," assured Mel. She looked at Kristy with a twinkle in her eye. "But we have decided I'm going to attend the community college this fall."

Kristy's heart leaped in her chest. She opened her mouth, but Leah clicked her tongue. "Do you really think it's safe to put so much stress on your body while you're pregnant? Especially with the bleeding."

"I haven't had any more trouble. I'm going to rest like the doctor said, but I should be fine when the fall semester starts," said Mel.

"Of course she'll be fine, and my Mel can handle whatever stress comes her way." Kristy fought to keep her voice low and her pitch even. "She's one of the strongest young ladies I know."

Mel beamed at her mom's praise, and Kristy realized she genuinely meant what she'd said. Mel was smart, and she was strong. Since finding out about the pregnancy, she'd determined to give her mistakes over to God. Like Timothy in the New Testament, Mel had a lot of wisdom, and Kristy praised God she was going to college.

Wade melted butter in a large pot and then added diced carrots, onion and celery, along with some salt and thyme. He stirred while the vegetables softened in the pot. The last thing he'd planned to do on the Fourth of July was make chicken noodle soup. And yet here he was.

He'd called Kristy earlier to see if she'd like to go to the rookie league baseball game at the Surprise Recreation Campus, but she'd been up the whole night before with a stomach bug. She'd sounded so groggy and weak that he'd headed straight to the store for the ingredients for the soup his grandma had always fixed to make him feel better when he was a kid.

Adding broth to the vegetables and seasoning, he turned up the heat until the soup boiled. He added egg noodles and set the timer for five minutes. Once the pasta was tender, he added cooked chicken and some cayenne and salt and pepper. Turning the heat to simmer, he cleaned up the kitchen and then took Bo for a walk around the neighborhood.

Once back at the house, he scratched Bo behind the ears. "We'll go to the dog park tomorrow."

He grabbed a couple sleeves of saltine crackers and the warm soup and headed to the car. When he reached Kristy's home, his heartbeat sped up. Today would be the first time he'd seen her since he'd admitted his true feelings to himself. He hadn't said them aloud, but what if they were somehow written into his expression? What if she didn't feel the same way?

Rolling his eyes at his own insecurity, he knocked on the front door. He wasn't some high school student with a teenage crush. He was a forty-year-old man. Kristy's minister. The one who guided her and the rest of the church members to a closer relationship with God.

His stomach flipped with new anxiety. If she didn't feel the same way and he shared his feelings, his admission would make things very challenging for both of them. She might not want to attend a church where the minister had fallen head over heels in love with her.

What am I thinking, Lord? He started to turn around,

but his conscience kept his feet planted. He couldn't run away now. He'd already knocked. Already heard shuffling inside the house. *Get yourself together. You'll just give her the soup as a concerned brother in Christ. Then you'll hightail it out of here.*

The door opened to a pale, puffy-eyed Kristy, with brown hair sticking out at odd angles around her head. "Wade?" she mumbled as she trailed her fingers through her wild mane. "What are you doing here?"

He held the pot higher, and the bag holding the crackers swayed back and forth from his wrist. "Brought you some soup."

A low groan seeped from her lips. "I don't want you to see me like this."

"What? You look great."

Kristy's eyes widened, and she grabbed her stomach and ran away from the door. Wade pursed his lips. What should he do now? The poor woman was obviously making a mad dash for the bathroom. With a shrug, he decided he couldn't leave the soup on the porch, so he let himself into the house. He took the pot and crackers to the kitchen. Moments later, Kristy appeared in the doorway, wearing a pink robe and an Arizona Razorbacks ball cap.

He chuckled as he pointed to her head. "A hat?"

She snarled, "My hair's a wreck. What's a girl supposed to do when her good-looking, single pastor comes to visit and she's been retching all night?"

His insides warmed that she found him attractive *and* that she wanted to look good for him. Maybe she shared his feelings after all. At least to some degree. He glanced around the kitchen. "Do you need anything? Some lemon-lime soda or an energy drink?"

She scrunched her nose. "I hate to ask you."

"That's what I'm here for."

"I'm dying for something bland and fizzy to settle down this queasiness."

Wade lifted his keys. "You got it. I'll be back in five minutes."

Making a straight dash to the convenience store a few blocks away, he picked up a twelve-pack of soda and a few different flavors of sports beverages, then drove back to Kristy's house. He knocked on the door again. This time, Carrie answered. A full smile covered her face. "Come on in, Pastor Wade." She opened the door wide. "I couldn't believe it when I walked in and smelled the delicious scent of homemade chicken noodle soup." She lifted her eyebrows. "Only someone who truly cares about a person makes homemade."

A nervous chuckle escaped his lips. He had nowhere to hide, and no one who would walk up and interrupt any questions Carrie might have. "Where's Kristy?"

"She's trying to clean up a bit." She pointed to a sack of groceries sitting on the coffee table. "I came over to warm up a couple cans of soup. Make sure my sister was comfortable. Never expected someone would beat me to it."

Wade shuffled his feet. He'd placed himself in an unfamiliar, awkward position. He'd always loved his church family and worked hard to encourage and teach them to follow the Lord, but he'd also kept any potential girlfriends at arm's length. Until Kristy.

Carrie intertwined her fingers and rocked back on her heels. "All teasing aside, I'm glad you care about her."

Before Wade could respond, Kristy called for her sister from the other room. He waited until Carrie came back to the living room. "She's still feeling pretty sick. I'm going to make her a bowl of your soup and take it to her bedroom."

"I can stay and help."

"She doesn't want you to see her like this."

"But—"

"Pastor Wade." Carrie pushed him toward the door. "Let me spell it out for you. When you first start really caring about someone, you don't want them to see you barfing all over the place. Do you understand?"

Excitement stirred within him. She did like him. He nodded as he turned to the door. "I'll just call her later."

"Perfect."

With the entire holiday open, Wade took Bo to the dog park, grilled hamburgers for one on his back deck and then watched fireworks from the backyard. Having thought and prayed for Kristy all day, he called her when the fireworks ended.

"How are you feeling?" he asked.

"Much better." She still sounded weak but nowhere near as groggy. "Your soup was wonderful."

"Thanks." *Just spit it out. You're too old to spend your days and nights thinking about her but never doing anything about it.* "I wondered if you'd be willing to go to dinner and a movie with me. When you feel better, of course."

"I thought you'd never ask."

Chapter 16

Kristy studied her reflection in the full-length mirror on the back of her bedroom door. She wore a denim-colored plain cotton sundress with a square-cut neckline. Though she'd had the dress for several years, she'd added a large yellow flower clip to one corner at the top and a thin white belt around her waist. The yellow-and-white wedges she'd bought at a clearance sale at one of her favorite shoe stores matched perfectly.

After trailing her fingertips through her short waves of hair, she pinched her cheeks. She might need to add a bit more blush. Though she felt better after spending a day vegging out in front of the television after her awful bout with the stomach bug, her complexion was still pale.

Carrie had called more times than Kristy could count since her big sister had shared the news of a first, official date. Thankfully, Mel had left the house early to spend the day with a few of her bridesmaids. She had no idea of her mother's plans for the evening.

The doorbell rang, and after one last glance at the mirror and a long exhale, she headed for the door. *It's okay. First date you've gone on in more years than you'd like to think about, but you can do this. It's just your pastor.*

The thought made her want to race back to her bedroom and slam the door. She shook her head and willed the fluttering butterflies to flit out of her stomach. *Too late for that.*

She opened the door. Wade looked handsome in a navy blue polo shirt and khaki pants. A full smile spread across his newly shaved face. She bit her bottom lip when she saw the bouquet of red, orange and yellow roses in his hands.

"You look beautiful, Kristy," he said, and then his face flushed like a young teen going on his first date. He handed her the flowers.

"These are lovely." She motioned him inside. "Come in. I'll put them in a vase, then we'll be on our way."

A memory of one of the first times Mel and Joel had gone out raced through her mind. He'd brought her a bouquet of wildflowers, which Kristy had deemed very sweet. Mel had giggled and then pulled her phone out of her purse. "Come on," she'd said. "We'll take a selfie with them, and I'll post it online."

Kristy bit back a chuckle. She wondered what Wade would think if she asked him to take a selfie. Pushing the silly thought away, she fixed the flowers, grabbed her purse and then followed him out the door. Like a true gentleman, he opened her car door and waited until she'd slipped inside before walking around to the driver's side.

"Where are we going?" she asked.

"Does a steak house sound all right?"

She patted her stomach. "Sounds delicious. I'm ready to eat again."

He chuckled but didn't respond. He seemed as nervous as she felt. She racked her brain for something to say. She liked him. Really liked him. But she didn't know how to date. She could count on two hands, maybe even one hand, how many dates she'd been on since Mel was born.

Once at the restaurant and seated, she picked up the menu and tried to peruse her choices. Wade pulled his smartphone out of his pocket and looked at something. She chewed the inside of her cheek. What if he hadn't really wanted to ask her out? Carrie was always hinting and teasing. Maybe she'd said something to him while Kristy was sick to make him feel as though he should. The butterflies in her stomach fluttered once more.

"Shaky, uptight, jittery, uneasy, apprehensive, overwrought." He looked up from his phone. "I was looking for a big, impressive word to express how nervous I am right now, but my phone isn't listing any."

Kristy smiled. "*Nervous* explains my feelings quite accurately."

"It sounds as though we're both being a little silly. We've been together many times before."

"Never on a date."

"True." His gaze penetrated hers as his expression softened. "But I'm really glad we're on one now."

Before Kristy could respond, the waitress arrived and took their orders. To be extracautious, she ordered a lemon-lime soda instead of a caffeinated soft drink. They passed the waitress the menus, then Wade clasped his hands and rested them on the table. "Tell me about yourself, Kristy."

She laughed again. "I think you know a lot about me already."

"Not *your* hopes and dreams. I'm wondering about what *you* want, not what you want for Mel."

She pursed her lips. Mel had been her hopes and dreams for so long she wasn't sure what she wanted. What God wanted for her. A sudden feeling of freedom overwhelmed her. She wasn't tied down to her expectations and goals for Mel. She didn't have to live her life through her daughter. "I'd always thought I wanted to be a prestigious English professor at a major university, but I really enjoy my position at the community college. I don't make a lot of money, but it's been enough to support me and Mel. Plus I'm able to help out at church a lot."

Wade nodded. "I know I appreciate your levelheadedness in our committee meetings. What about the future?"

"We heard the baby's heartbeat at Mel's last doctor's appointment." A sudden excitement swelled in her chest. "Her pregnancy might not be the ideal start, but babies are always blessings, and I find I'm already excited to meet the little guy or girl."

"What about you? Not Mel. Not the baby. Not even the church. You."

Kristy tilted her head. "Anyone ever tell you that you have tunnel vision?"

"Maybe."

She furrowed her brows as her mind raced for an answer. "You know what? I don't know. Whatever God has for me, I suppose."

Wade had asked Kristy to go to dinner and a movie with him, but then he'd had another idea after he'd asked for the check. Apprehension swelled in his gut as he drove closer to the destination. Part of him feared she'd think him too forward. Acting more like her committed boyfriend or husband instead of her date. But this was more than a date. They'd spent time together already, and he wanted to give her something. Do something just for her.

He parked in front of a dress shop. Kristy looked to her left, then her right. "Why are we here?"

"I'm assuming you need a mother-of-the-bride dress."

"What?" Kristy leaned back in the passenger's seat and pressed her hand against her chest.

He cringed. "I probably should have asked if you'd bought one already. I didn't even think of that."

"I haven't purchased anything." Kristy shook her head. "But I don't understand. I thought we were going to a movie."

"We can if you want to, but…" He shrugged, searching for the right words to say. Since his run-in with Wilma on the Waddell Trail at White Tank Mountains and his full surrender to forgive himself for Zella's death, God had been speaking to his heart in an almost shouting voice. Scripture had come alive. His desire to love and serve and help had never been so strong. He no longer operated on his own strength, but had given every aspect of his life to the Lord. He cleared his throat. "I'd like to buy your dress for you."

Kristy frowned. "Why?"

"The wedding and pregnancy have been such a surprise, and I'm impressed with how you've handled yourself with Mel and Leah and Joel. Just everyone. I respect you, and I've grown to care about you." *Finally allowed myself to fall in love with you.* He withheld the last thought. "I just want to do this for you."

"I don't think that's appropriate, Wade."

"Why not?"

She lifted her hands. "Oh, I don't know. We're not married. You're my pastor. Do I need more reasons?"

"We're not living in the Stone Age, Kristy. I hardly think my buying you a dress is inappropriate."

She cocked her head. "For a smart guy, you are really naive when it comes to boy-girl relationships."

"I'm just trying to help. Isn't that the Christian thing to do?"

"So you're buying the dress because I'm a struggling single mom?"

Wade shrugged. "I suppose."

"So you're gonna buy Eustace's dress? She's a single woman on a fixed budget."

Wade's face and neck warmed. "Well, no. It's just…"

"Just what, Wade?"

"I want to do this." He tapped the top of the steering wheel. "I need to help you somehow."

"Why?"

"I care about you, Kristy."

She cocked her head and studied him for what seemed an eternity. He'd have loved to know what she was thinking. Finally, she whispered, "I've been saving money for this already, but if I go overbudget, you can help. Okay."

They walked into the shop and perused the dresses. She turned to him with a playful look. "What would you think a fancy dress costs these days?"

He hadn't thought of that. What did a mother-of-the-bride dress cost? He hoped not more than a hundred. He glanced at the nearest price tag and held back a gasp. No. Obviously, they could cost a great deal more than that.

Seeming to read his thoughts, Kristy's lips curled into a teasing smile. "The last time I was in a dress shop, Leah told Mel her limit was seven *thousand*."

Wade coughed, and Kristy laughed out loud. She grabbed his hand, and electricity shot up his arm when her fingers wrapped around his. "Let's head to the back, where they have sales. If we can't find anything, we'll hit the mall."

The dresses in the back were much more reasonably priced, and Wade sighed with relief. "Does the color matter?"

"Her wedding colors are hot pink and purple. Since the bridesmaids are wearing both colors, I thought I'd get a pastel version of either one."

Though he felt a little weird and completely out of his element, he pulled a light pinkish dress off the rack. "This looks pretty."

Kristy lifted her brows. "That dress is way too small for me."

"What size do you wear?"

She blew out a breath. "As if I'm going to tell you that." She pointed to a padded bench to the side. "You just have a seat right there. I'll go through the dresses."

After what seemed like hours, Kristy turned back to him with a ridiculous amount of satin and lacy clothing draped over her arm. She tilted her head. "Are you sure you want to sit here while I try on all these dresses?"

He smacked his hands against his thighs. "I wanna see every one of 'em, too."

"Okay." Kristy winked. "But you're asking for it."

An hour passed. He had looked at every shape and style of dress ever created. Who'd have thought there could be so many pinks and purples in the world? Every dress was either too short or too long. Too young or too old. Too loose or too stiff. He had no idea a person could feel so many things and experience so many concerns when trying to purchase a single item of clothing.

He understood why men didn't shop with women. Why comedians wrote jokes about the experience. He was being tortured. Plain and simple. He'd even suggested it. Scratching his jaw, he realized he'd seen many women in the store.

Young and old. But not a single man. Every other male on the planet had more sense than he did.

She opened the door to the fitting room. Like almost every other gown she'd tried on, she looked amazing. "What do you think?"

He clasped his hands. "You look terrific. I think we could get you a potato sack and you'd look great."

She narrowed her gaze, then grinned. "That sounded a tad sarcastic. Is someone getting a little tired of looking at dresses?"

"No," he lied, then thought of his last sermon and how he'd encouraged the church to speak the truth in love. He shook his head back and forth. "Okay, maybe I'm a little bit tired."

Kristy feigned a hurt expression, but the twinkle in her eyes proved her teasing. She turned back to the mirror and then flipped the piece of ruffled fabric at the top. "I don't like the lace here." She looked at him. "Let me try on just one more."

"I told you I'm fine."

While she changed again, he scrolled through the apps on his phone. He'd used up all his lives in every silly game he'd downloaded to the electronic device. Clicking it off, he shoved the phone in his pocket, then tapped his fingers on the top of the bench.

"How about this one?"

She wore a light pink dress that touched the top of her knees. The shoulder straps were probably two inches wide and the neck dropped down in a V shape. A pretty glittery silver belt-like design wrapped around her small waist. But it wasn't a belt. It was more like a decoration. Whatever it was, she looked beautiful. "It's perfect."

"I think this is the one."

"But it seems as if I already saw it."

"It's the first one I tried on."

Wade dipped his chin and glared at her. "Are you kidding me?"

"Nope." She chuckled. "Are you ever going shopping with me again?"

"Probably not."

She pouted. "So you wish you'd never offered?"

Wade stood and shoved his hands into his pockets. He knew she was teasing, but her expression sent his senses into overdrive. He wanted to wrap his arms around her and press his lips against her pouty ones. He nodded to the door. "You just go change back into your clothes. We'll get the dress, then head for some ice cream."

She disappeared back into the dressing room.

And if he could muster the courage, he might sneak in a good-night kiss.

Chapter 17

He still hadn't kissed her. Kristy shoved her laptop in the briefcase and zipped it up. She'd been sure Wade would kiss her when he'd taken her home from their date on Saturday. For the second time, she'd even leaned in a bit when he'd walked her to the front door so that he'd know she was willing. Instead, he'd yanked his keys out of his front pocket and walked to his car.

She'd had trouble focusing on his sermon the next morning and, when they'd talked a few moments after church, had needed to squash the never-leaving butterflies in her stomach. He hadn't called or texted since then. Sure, it wasn't even quite Monday afternoon, but they'd had a good time on Saturday night.

At least, she'd had a good time. The hour in the dress shop might have been a bit much for him. Again, she chuckled, remembering his expression when he'd seen the original price tags of the dresses in the front of the store.

He'd tried to act excited about each dress, but she'd caught him more than once playing a game on his smartphone.

She walked out the front double doors of the community college. The hot July air actually felt nice after leaving the frigid classroom. She'd almost reached her car door when someone grabbed her arm, and she made a fist with her other hand.

"You're being kidnapped."

Kristy blew out her breath and flexed her fingers. "Wade. You just gave me a heart attack. You're lucky I didn't punch you."

"I'm glad you didn't." He lifted up a red tote bag she recognized as her own. "Come on. You're going with me."

"And just where are we going?"

"Fishing. Surprise Lake."

Kristy snorted. "I haven't fished since I was a kid. I don't have a fishing license, and—"

Wade placed his finger on her lips, and she sucked in her breath. "We're going to get your license right now. I have a picnic lunch ready for us, and Mel packed some casual clothes for you."

She raised her eyebrows. "Aren't you prepared for everything."

"I told you. I'm kidnapping you." He gently tugged her arm. "Now go get in my car."

Feigning frustration, she traipsed to his vehicle. He opened her door, and she slid into the passenger's seat. He got in behind the wheel. They drove to a local store, and he purchased her license while she changed in the public restroom. She grimaced as she shimmied and twisted in an effort not to touch the stall walls or place her bare feet on the concrete floor. Wade was the only person who'd be able to convince her to do this, as she used public facilities only when absolutely necessary. And changing clothes in a store bathroom should *never* be necessary.

Dressed and ready to go, she stepped out of the bathroom, and Wade waved a paper in the air. "Your license is taken care of. Let's go."

Kristy plastered a smile to her face. This was just the kind of date she'd always dreamed of: stabbing an innocent worm with a hook and then yanking up a slimy, smelly fish a few minutes later. But then she had to admit she kind of owed him. Their first date had been a fashion show of Kristy, so she supposed she could survive an afternoon of fishing.

At the park, she asked Wade what she could do to help him set up their lunch, but he refused any assistance. While he placed a vinyl tablecloth on the picnic table, she picked at her fingernails. Watching him take a bucket of fried chicken, mashed potatoes and coleslaw from a large container, she decided right then that she would get a kiss from Wade today. Even if she had to do it herself.

He pulled a small container of sweet tea as well as individually wrapped strawberry cheesecakes from a cooler. "Okay, I think we're ready. It's all from a fast-food restaurant, but it's still one of my favorite meals."

"Looks good to me." She pressed her palm against her stomach. "I haven't eaten in hours."

Wade motioned for her to have a seat on one side of the picnic table, then he sat down across from her. He took her hands in his and said a blessing over their meal. When he looked up, he sucked in a big breath and then exhaled. Standing, he walked back over to her and took her hand, lifting it until she stood.

"I've gotta do this before I lose my nerve."

Before she could figure out his meaning, Wade leaned down and pressed his lips against hers. He started to lift his head after a quick peck, but Kristy wrapped her arms around his neck and pulled him closer. Eagerly, he claimed her lips again and then deepened the kiss.

Fireworks seemed to explode in her chest, in her mind, all over her. She hadn't kissed a man in decades, and Wade's soft yet urgent lips made her head spin.

He pulled away from her. His blue eyes smoldered with a fire she hoped one day to ignite into a full flame. "Wow," he whispered.

She touched his cheek with her palm, loving the feel of his coarse stubbles. "It's about time."

The week had been one of the best Wade could recall. Every time he opened God's word, some truth or encouragement jumped off the page and into his heart. He was on fire to preach and teach the Bible.

And he'd found reasons to see and kiss Kristy every day. One night, they'd watched a movie together at her house. Another, they'd taken Bo to the dog park. After Wednesday-night church service, they'd gotten ice cream. On Thursday, they'd shared coffee. Another evening, they'd had an official date, another nice restaurant. They'd even exercised in the gym together one afternoon.

He made his way into the music minister's office before the Sunday-morning service. Chad was tuning his guitar, his expression one of concern.

"Worried about the songs this morning?" asked Wade.

Chad huffed. "That's an understatement."

"I picked them out. You can blame me."

Chad grinned as he scratched his beard. "Oh, I will. Don't you worry."

Wade laughed, and Chad pointed to the bulletin. "Seriously, this is a good worship lineup for now. Start with a contemporary version of an older hymn, segue to a faster contemporary praise song and then sing a hymn before you preach."

"I'm hoping it will be a good compromise." Wade studied his new friend. "You're worried about the guitar, aren't you?"

Chad placed his palm against the guitar's belly. "I mean, I know it's not like we're adding drums, but they're so used to only having the piano."

"Becca's playing the piano as well, right?"

"Yeah."

"The best thing to ease our fears is to pray about it. We'll pray the Holy Spirit will lead the music and that the church will be receptive to Him. Worship is about Him, not us."

After a quick prayer, Chad seemed more confident, and Wade felt a covering of peace. They made their way to the sanctuary and started the service. God's presence filled the church. The faces of both young and old members shone with praise. Wade preached the scriptures God had shown him earlier in the week. As he shook hands with the congregation at the end of the service, many expressed pleasure with the music.

Feeling good about their committee meeting later that afternoon but exhausted from a busy week, he went home and took a short nap before heading back to church. He walked into their meeting room and was surprised to see Greg and Freddy sitting beside each other, talking about Freddy's teenage grandson. Becca and Kristy sat together. He wasn't sure what they were discussing, but Kristy's face flushed when she smiled at him. He sat down in an open chair. "Has anyone seen Eustace?"

"I'm sure she'll be here. She and Dortha were yakking on the phone just a little bit ago," boomed Freddy.

Wade clasped his hands and rested them on the table.

"I received a lot of positive feedback from the congregation about the music. What did you all think?"

"I loved it," said Becca.

"Definitely," added Greg. "I, personally, enjoy more contemporary, but I thought it was a terrific balance for our church."

Freddy patted Greg's back. "I'd have to agree with Greg. My grandson even said he'd come back tonight for youth."

Wade looked at Kristy, and she shifted in her seat. "You know I liked it."

"Well, I hated it."

All heads turned at the sound of Eustace's voice. She glowered as she entered the room and plopped down in the chair beside Kristy. "I hated it," she said again.

"Okay. What did you hate?" asked Wade.

"The only good part was the hymn." She pointed her finger at Becca. "Her husband shouldn't be bringing a guitar into the Sunday-morning worship service. It ain't right."

Becca sat up straighter and lifted her chin. "And who decided 'it ain't right'? You? Where in the Bible did God say not to have a guitar in worship?"

"It's a slippery slope," Eustace spat out.

Wade touched each woman's forearm to keep his two congregants from waging a full-blown war. He studied the older woman. She seemed especially tired and worn. He recognized the look, because though he was decades younger than her, he'd seen the same signs on his own face. She was battling something. Not a cold or a physical ailment. She had a spiritual war raging inside her. "Eustace, you have a right to your opinion. Tell us what else you didn't like."

"We shouldn't have fast music in worship. It ain't right." She waved her hand. "These young people come in and just want to change everything, when we've worshipped

God just fine for years with the old songs." She motioned to Freddy. "Even Dortha said she didn't like the music."

Freddy puffed out his chest. "Now, wait a minute, Eustace. I know that's not true. The woman even made me listen to some contemporary-Christian music station on the way home." He looked around the table. "I suppose it wasn't all bad."

Eustace huffed. The committee continued to talk, and Wade made a list of things they liked and didn't like about the program. Eustace seemed determined to challenge every positive remark. Even with her objection, the members agreed to try the same format again the next week. When Wade closed in prayer, he followed Eustace out of the room.

"Is everything all right?"

"What?" she snapped. "Just because I disagree with you that means something is wrong?"

"You just seem upset."

She waved her hand. "Of course I'm upset. I'm being forced to listen to awful music during my worship service."

Before he could comment, she hustled away from him. More than just music was bothering Eustace. He'd make it a point to pray for her, pray that God would give her peace and joy that could come from only Him.

Chapter 18

Kristy glanced at the two hundred mini succulent plants in small white pots that stretched across most of the deck in her backyard. She wrinkled her nose and turned to Carrie. "How did I get stuck with this job?"

"You're the mom."

Kristy huffed. "I've had a say in very few things for this wedding." She pointed to her chest. "I said party favors for the guests was a bit extravagant."

Carrie rocked Noah side to side and patted his bottom as he fought taking a nap. "But Leah felt they were necessary."

Kristy nodded in exaggerated motions. "Exactly. And as such, don't you think she should fix these things?"

"I don't think it works that way." Carrie pointed to the only completed plant. "This is what it's supposed to look like?"

"Yep. She made sure I had an example, since I'm not overly crafty."

Carrie snorted. "You have the worst crafting abilities I've ever seen."

"Hey!"

"Let's face it. You can barely get the tape off the dispenser."

Kristy held up a pile of cellophane pieces. "That might be why she went ahead and cut these out."

"The paper is already cut?"

"Ribbon, too."

"What are you complaining about? Just wrap up the plants and be done with it."

"Fine."

Kristy picked up a plant and set it in the center of one of the cellophane pieces.

"I think she used two," said Carrie.

Kristy glared at her. "You just rock my nephew and leave the decorating to me."

Realizing her sister was right, Kristy picked up a second piece and put it on top of the first. She lifted each side around the pot, but when she tried to wrap the ribbon around it, a corner of the cellophane popped out. Pursing her lips, she tried placing the paper in her hand, then putting the pot in the center of her palm. She tried to shimmy the ribbon from the bottom, but she needed both hands to make the cellophane even on both sides of the plant.

"Oh, for crying out loud, take the baby." Carrie sighed. She rolled her eyes as she shoved Noah into Kristy's arms.

Kristy cuddled her nephew to her chest, then wrapped his light receiving blanket around his body. She jostled him gently and rubbed his back until he'd fallen asleep in her arms. She kissed the top of his downy head and whispered, "I'd rather be good at cuddling babies than crafting anyway."

She looked back at her sister. Carrie had already finished wrapping five plants in purple cellophane tied with hot pink bows. "I can't believe you've done those so fast."

"It's really not that hard, sis."

She scrunched up her face and mocked her sister. "I've made it this long without making crafts, I suppose I'll make it a little longer."

"You just keep holding my little monster."

"Is he still not sleeping well?"

"Six weeks old and still wakes up every few hours at night."

Kristy grazed her finger across his soft forehead. "He's a little guy. He'll get there."

"I hope so. I'm exhausted, and I'm worried he'll keep Mom and Dad awake when they get here next week."

"Are you kidding? You're probably going to get two weeks of a full night's sleep. They'll probably scoop him up out of his crib before you have a chance to realize he's peeped."

Carrie threw back her head. "Sounds wonderful."

Mel stepped onto the deck. "Mom, the bridal shop just called. My dress is ready." She waved at Carrie. "Oh, hi, Aunt Carrie." She chuckled. "Mom recruited you to do the party favors?"

"Your mother is the baby whisperer. I am the craft…" She tilted her head and furrowed her brows.

"Putter-togetherer," said Kristy.

Carrie clicked her tongue. "And to think you're the English professor."

"I'm going to take a shower, but I wanna go pick up the dress tonight. You gotta go with me."

"Okay," said Kristy. "Let me know when you're ready."

Carrie continued to decorate the succulent plants. "No more scares, huh?"

"No." Kristy sighed. "Thank the Lord. She scared me

to death that night. Eustace made a few snide innuendos at our meeting last week, though."

"What do you think is up with that? I mean, she's always been a gossip, but she's never been so mean about everything. She even got up and walked out during Becca's solo at church."

Kristy looked out past her backyard at the setting sun. A thick yellow ring surrounded the almost-white sphere. An orange hue spread out away from the sun, as far as she could see. "I don't know what's wrong. I've been trying to pray for her."

"That whole 'being kind to your enemies to heap lumps of coal on them'?"

"No." Kristy chuckled. "When did you get so vicious?"

"I'm the baby of the family. I've always been mean."

"No. I genuinely want to pray for her peace." Noah stirred and threw out his arm. She tucked it back close to her. He made small sucking faces and then drifted back to sleep. "It's just hard to feel what I'm praying sometimes."

"Guess that's why we can't trust our hearts."

Mel opened the back door again. "Mom, I'm ready."

Carrie motioned to the playpen. "Lay him down, and I'll finish up these wedding favors."

"You sure?"

"What? You're gonna finish them?"

"If I didn't have this baby in my arms, I'd flick you in the head."

"Then I'd have to pull out the big guns." Carrie lifted her arms and kissed her biceps.

Mel shook her head. "You two are crazy."

Once she'd laid down Noah, Kristy nudged Mel to the door. "Come on. We better hurry. I haven't checked my email today to see what other things Leah has planned for me."

* * *

Wade folded the corner of the purple napkin over the bottom of the knife, fork and spoon. Next, he folded one corner around the front to the back and then did the same for the other side. Taking a piece of thick pink ribbon with purple polka dots, he wrapped it around the center of the silverware and then tied a bow in the front.

"You've got to be kidding me," Kristy whined. She raised her hands. "Listen. I can read you a book. Write you an article. I can rock a baby. Clean a house. But I cannot do this crafty stuff."

"I think you're just psyching yourself out. You can do it." He picked up another set of silverware, a napkin and a ribbon. "Do exactly what I do."

He followed the same steps, stopping to be sure she did everything he had done. After she tied a somewhat crooked bow in the front, she clapped. "I did it."

"I knew you could."

"Let me follow you again. Just to be sure."

They wrapped more sets of silverware, and Kristy continued to copy his every move. His feelings for her deepened each time he saw her, and his walk with the Lord had grown in ways he hadn't expected. Though he was saved by grace, he hadn't realized how thirsty he'd been for daily living water. He wanted more than just dating from Kristy, but he needed to be honest about his struggles first. "How is the wedding coming?"

"Terrific. Leah and I have actually gotten along well lately. She has strengths I simply don't have, and I've come to admire her for them." She raised her eyebrows as she lifted a completed set of silverware. "The wedding's going to be, by far, lovelier than anything I'd have come up with."

"Bigger than you expected?"

"Now, *that* I would like to do without."

"When are your parents coming?"

"Next week." She cocked her head. "Why do I get the feeling there's something you're not saying?"

"Actually, I do want to share something with you." He wiped his hands against his khaki shorts.

"You're not married or have kids somewhere, do you?"

"What?" He shook his head and blinked. "No. Why would you think that?"

"That's usually what happens on television."

He pursed his lips. "I want to tell you about my fiancée."

Kristy leaned back in her chair. A worried expression draped her features. "This is starting to sound a lot like what happens on television."

He furrowed his brows and wrinkled his nose. "When I was twenty, I was engaged to an amazing girl. Her name was Zella. She was beautiful and vibrant and excited to tell the whole world about Jesus. I was absolutely crazy about her."

Wade looked at Kristy. She'd crossed her arms. Her frown had shifted from worry to something he couldn't identify. He raked his fingers through his hair. He was botching up the whole thing.

"About a month before our wedding, we went for a drive and had a wreck."

Kristy sucked in her breath. He knew she understood where he was going now.

"I hit another car, and she died."

He'd expected her to embrace him, to say she was sorry for what had happened. Instead, she chewed her bottom lip and stared at him. "Why are you telling me this?"

He opened his arms. "Because I've been stuck there for two decades. Stuck in the guilt of her death. It wasn't until I moved to Surprise, preached a sermon on forgiveness and Wilma opened my eyes to the very words I'd spoken. Because I've finally forgiven myself, I'm able to move forward."

"I'm really glad," Kristy said, and this time she did lean forward and wrap her hand around his. "I've noticed a difference in you."

"Yes," he agreed. "I'm on fire again. I've never been so excited to study God's word, to learn and share more about His truths." He paused and swallowed the knot in his throat. "And able to love again."

"What are you saying?"

He moved his chair closer to hers and cupped her chin in his hands. "That I love you."

A slow smile spread across her lips as she whispered, "I love you, too."

He claimed her lips with his and relished the fire that burned in his heart and sent electricity down his veins at her touch. He released her, and she scratched the stubbles on his jaw with her fingertips. "For a preacher, you're a pretty good kisser."

"Oh, you've kissed a lot of preachers, huh?"

"Just one."

He placed a quick kiss on her lips again, then forced himself to return to wrapping silverware. Everything in him wanted to make her his bride right away. Today would be fine with him. But he didn't want to do anything to keep her from enjoying and focusing on Mel and Joel. But soon, he'd ask her to marry him.

Chapter 19

The Sunday-morning service had been awesome. They'd had several visitors, and Kristy had felt the Holy Spirit filling the church. Hiring Wade as the church's pastor had been the best decision ever. She was glad he was here.

After a leisurely lunch, they were returning for the committee meeting. He released her hand to open the church door for her.

She was overwhelmed with all they still needed to do for the wedding, but she couldn't believe how things had worked out. Leah had been a terrific wedding planner— and she had ample time and energy to devote to the nuptials. She'd thought of things Kristy would have never considered, and Kristy found herself starting to like Mel's stepmother. On some levels anyway. She still got a little jealous when she saw Mel get excited about something Leah put together, but that was her human nature, not what God wanted from her as a Christian.

"I really liked that new restaurant," Wade said as he took her hand again while they walked down the hall.

"Me, too." She smiled up at him as contentment swelled within her. Life couldn't get any more perfect. The summer had brought changes she would have never believed possible three months ago, but God had been faithful and consistent in every trial and challenge.

Wade opened the door to the room where the committee met. Greg, Freddy and Eustace already sat around the table. Eustace seemed more upset than she had been even a week ago. Kristy had prayed for the older woman many times over the past seven days. She knew God would want her to love Eustace despite her actions. Uncomfortable as she felt, she sat beside Eustace and offered her a hesitant smile. The older woman's response was to look away. *Okay, God. Help me to love. Jesus was nailed to a cross for my sins, and yet You love me. I can love a woman who just doesn't like me.*

Becca burst into the room and clapped her hands. "Today's service was amazing!"

"I couldn't believe all the visitors," Freddy boomed.

"God's presence was definitely with us," added Wade.

Greg tapped his finger against the table. "What's fantastic is we haven't taken away anyone's preferred style of music."

Wade nodded. "We still have hymns."

"And the contemporary," said Greg.

Freddy chortled. "I'm even beginning to appreciate some of the contemporary."

Greg nudged Freddy, a friendship Kristy would have never thought possible. "And I've found a new appreciation for the hymns."

Wade leaned back in the chair. "I'm not sure the committee has a purpose anymore." He looked at each of them. "Our job was to encourage unity."

Becca bounced in her seat. "And we're unified."

"Are we, now?" The words spit from Eustace's lips with a venom that curled Kristy's toes. The older woman pressed both hands flat against the table and peered at each of them. "So we're unified once we allow sin into our church?"

"Now, Eustace," said Freddy, "The music these kids like to listen to is not sinful. I've listened to it, and—"

"I'm not talking about the music," Eustace barked.

Wade frowned. "What are you talking about?"

Eustace pointed from him to Kristy, and Kristy's insides twisted. "The two of you seem to be getting quite friendly."

Kristy's face burned, and Wade opened his mouth to respond, but Greg piped up, "What's wrong with that?"

"She had a child out of wedlock."

The words slithered from Eustace's lips, and Kristy looked at her accuser. The anger and disappointment she'd felt all those years ago when she'd found out she was pregnant with Mel washed over her. The woman on the talk show's words floated through her mind. *No matter what I do, I'll always be a teenage-pregnancy statistic.*

Kristy needed to get up, to run away from the room and the humiliation, but her body remained frozen, glued to the chair.

"I can't believe you would say that." Becca's voice had risen to nearly a squeal.

"Eustace." Freddy's deep voice sounded mournful and sorry. "You've known Kristy for so many years. You know she's a woman of God who simply made a mistake. She's repented of her sin."

Kristy stared at the table. She couldn't look up. Couldn't bear to see the expressions on their faces. She loved Wade, but there were consequences to choices. Her choice all those years ago would always be a burden to a minister, and she wouldn't ask him to endure this ever again.

"Why do you think her daughter is marrying so quickly?" Disdain slipped through Eustace's teeth. "She's followed in her mother's footsteps. That's why."

Wade, Greg, Freddy and Becca all responded at once. Their words jumbled in Kristy's mind, and she forced her legs out of the chair and raced out of the room. Without a backward glance, she ran out of the church. Her fingers tore through her purse in a desperate search for her keys.

Becca's voice sounded behind her, but Kristy couldn't make out the words. She didn't want to anyway. She had to get out of there. Away from the accusations. Away from the memories.

She was a fool to think Wade could love her or that she could be a match for a man like him. The man had pledged his life to the Lord's work. He was a wonderful minister and a true man of God. His love for God and for people were like none she'd ever seen, which was probably why she'd fallen in love with him.

Tears coursed down her cheeks as she hopped into her car and peeled out of the parking lot. He deserved so much more than someone like her. She brought burdens and sins she could never get past. Ministers' wives should be women whose lives didn't scream of their past transgressions. She knew everyone sinned, pastors' wives included. But she didn't know a single one who'd had a child out of wedlock. Or a pastor whose teenaged stepdaughter had had a baby at eighteen. He'd have to constantly explain how all of them were related. He deserved more than that.

Afraid Mel would be home and see her in such a miserable state, she drove to the White Tank Mountains. She parked as far from other cars as she could and then stared at God's majestic creation. Her mind was a blank, and she prayed the Holy Spirit translated her heart's groaning to the Lord, as scripture said.

She could never run away from the past, and yet she never wanted to. Mel, her greatest blessing, had come from her sin. Now Mel had gotten pregnant. But she was marrying a man she truly loved—and going to college, too. It would be challenging, but Mel was strong.

Tears flowed faster down Kristy's cheeks. She didn't want her daughter to experience this guilt and condemnation. And yet soon enough, she would know some of what Kristy had experienced. No matter how many people understood or sympathized, she'd still know the guilt.

Greg had followed Becca out the door. Wade wanted to chase after them, to wrap Kristy in his arms and assure her that Eustace's cruelty was wrong, but he had to address the older woman first. Her negativity had become toxic to the congregation.

"Eustace," Freddy chided. "What is the matter with you? Something's not right. You're not this hardened. You're…"

Eustace lifted her chin and crossed her arms. A flash of regret swept through her gaze before a defiant glare took over her face.

Wade turned to Freddy. "Do you mind if I talk to Eustace for a minute? Just the two of us."

"Sure." Freddy stood and patted Wade's shoulder. "You're doing a great job, Pastor."

Eustace raised her chin just a tad higher. Wade was surprised she hadn't got up and walked away. Proof his gut feeling was right. He needed to talk with her.

"What is it?" He tapped his chest. "In here."

"Not a thing," she spat out as she shifted in the seat.

"Just don't think it's right for my pastor to be traipsing all over town with a never-married woman who has a kid who's having a baby out of wedlock."

She humphed and moved her shoulders side to side. "I'm sorry. She won't be out of wedlock. My pastor's going to marry the pregnant teen to her boyfriend."

Wade placed his elbows on the table, clasped his hands together and pressed his lips against his fists. He offered a silent prayer for God to guide his thoughts and words. "You're upset about more than that. You're angry." He inspected her countenance, the bitterness that seemed to seep from every part of her body. "Guilty."

He hadn't expected the word to slip out, but when it did, Eustace dipped her chin and slumped in the chair. She didn't speak, and Wade didn't pressure her. No questions. No comments. Something in him knew he needed to give her time. He'd wait for her to respond.

Eustace placed both hands on the table. She folded her left hand over the right, then her right hand over the left. Over and over, she wrung her hands together. Finally, she whispered, "You're right. I'm guilty."

"Whatever it is, God has forgiven you."

She peered up at him. "Really?" Sarcasm dripped from her words. "Is it that simple?"

"Forgiveness is that simple."

Eustace huffed, and a mocking laugh sounded from deep within her. "Maybe for God. Definitely not for us."

Wade allowed silence to drape over them once again. He prayed God would show him what to say. A scripture from Colossians sprang into his mind, like a blinking hotel light offering weary travelers rest for the night. "'Bear with each other and forgive one another,'" he began, "'if any of you has a grievance against someone.'"

"'Forgive as the Lord forgave you.'" Eustace finished

the verse. She furrowed her brows. "Do you think I don't know my scriptures? The only reason I've survived these past fifty-five years is because of them."

"Then you know God's mercy," Wade implored. "A sin, once forgiven, is remembered no more."

"You're wrong," Eustace whispered as tears sprang to her eyes and then rolled down her cheeks.

Wade got up, grabbed a box of tissues from another table and gave them to Eustace. Again, he waited while she cried. Inwardly, he battled whether he should hug her or pat her hand or simply let her cry. After a sniff and a dab to her eyes, she said, "I can't forget my baby."

Understanding dawned within him, and with it, a wave of sorrow.

"He was fifty-five a few weeks ago. That's all I know about him. His day of birth, and he's a boy."

She crossed her arms, wrapping her hands around her upper arms as if she was cold. "My parents were furious when they discovered my pregnancy. They sent me away to my aunt and uncle's house. When the child was born, they took him away. I never even got to hold him."

Though he didn't speak, his mind wondered if she'd tried to leave her parents. Possibly get help from the father of the child. As if reading his thoughts, she said, "My boyfriend and I were only fifteen. I never saw him again."

She pushed away from the table, stood and paced around the room. "My parents never took me back into their home. I never married because I knew my future husband deserved more than a tainted wife. And I never told a soul."

Wade turned toward her. "No matter how your family responded, Eustace, you're—"

"Forgiven," she said. She shook her head and balled her fists. "I know." She pointed to her head. "In my mind, I know that, but I've never been able to live it. I wanted to keep my baby so badly…"

She moved across the room again and then waved her hand toward him. "You preached that sermon on forgiveness, and Wilma just went cuckoo because she was finally able to forgive herself for smoking in front of Ron." She lifted her hand higher. "Every time we got together, she went on and on about how her heart felt pounds lighter." She chuckled, but the sound was bitter and angry. "And it's true, she's been a lot healthier."

"You can have that, too," Wade said.

"I've tried." She shrugged. "Doesn't work. I can't forget my son. I don't even want to. I wondered about his teething, when he potty trained, how his first day of kindergarten went…"

"Let's try this a different way." Wade patted the chair to encourage her to sit beside him again. He pointed to his chest. "It's true the heart can be difficult, but I don't know that you need to forget your child."

Eustace sat down. "Forgive and forget. Isn't that what we're called to do?"

Wade tapped his Bible. "God forgets our sins, but I don't think any of us ever do. Remembering and knowing what we've done wrong keeps us from repeating the sin. Maybe you'd find forgiveness for yourself by being an encouragement to those who've experienced what you have."

She sat still, and he couldn't tell if she was contemplating his words or had started stewing with frustration again. He remembered what Kristy had shared about her feelings of guilt, and his heart hurt for Eustace, that she'd tortured herself for so long with shame that had never come from God.

"People fail every day, Eustace. Even Christians like your parents."

Eustace let out a slow breath and covered her face with her palm. "I can't believe I said those things to Kristy. I have become just like the people who hurt me so deeply. I should have understood better."

"The good news is that I think you can fix it. I have an idea."

Chapter 20

Kristy picked up the buzzing smartphone and clicked the decline button once again. A mature person would break off a relationship face-to-face. But if she saw him, or if he tried to kiss her, she would melt and agree to anything he said. The least she could do was answer his calls, but she didn't have the strength to hear his voice. True love was doing what was best for the other person, and she was not good for Wade.

"I can hardly wait for them to get off the plane." Carrie cradled a sleeping Noah closer to her chest. "Mom is gonna absolutely flip over this little guy."

"Mom?" Kristy teased. "You mean Dad. The poor guy had to raise three daughters and then got stuck with only a granddaughter for eighteen years."

"Hey," Mel squealed. "I heard that."

Kristy brushed a quick kiss on Noah's downy head. "If Kaitlyn was here, the homecoming would be perfect."

"I know," Carrie said. "I don't think we're ever all going to be together at one time."

"Gets harder as everyone gets older and chooses their own paths." Kristy glanced at her daughter, thankful she and Joel would be living just across town from her.

"Looks as though we still have a few minutes before the plane lands." Carrie checked the arrivals board near baggage claim then sat on the bench beside Mel. "How's the wedding coming?"

"Ugh," Mel moaned and rolled her eyes. "Leah's driving me crazy." She waved her hand. "I'm to the point that I told her just to do whatever she wants. I don't even care."

"She's worked really hard, and everything I've seen looks beautiful."

Carrie lifted her eyebrows and dipped her chin at Kristy's defense of Mel's stepmom.

Mel stomped her foot. "Yeah, but the wedding is more about her than me and Joel. Over a hundred of our guests are people we don't know. Friends of hers and Dad's." She widened her eyes and bobbed her head. "Over a hundred."

Carrie shrugged. "At least you'll get lots of great gifts."

Mel clicked her tongue and chuckled. "Good point. Hadn't thought of that."

Kristy looked around at the people racing from one destination to another. Many wore T-shirts proclaiming the various locations they'd traveled from. She watched as a young woman adjusted two babies in a double stroller. A man carrying a briefcase and talking on a cell phone brushed past her. Rat race. That was what the airport reminded her of. So many people with so many plans and destinations, all running one way or another.

Her phone buzzed again, and she pressed the decline button once more. Opening a text, she typed, I won't answer. I won't be a stumbling block for you.

As she expected, Wade responded right away. Using all the determination she could muster, she ignored the text. It wouldn't take much for her to run back to him, but a relationship with her was not what he needed.

She wrinkled her nose. She'd have to figure out what to do about church once the wedding was over. No way was she going to attend where he preached. She'd miss the people. Well, maybe not Eustace. She gritted her teeth. There was only so much "praying for your enemies" that she could endure. But that wasn't her only dilemma. What reason would she give Mel for worshipping somewhere else?

"Somebody's deep in thought," said Carrie.

Kristy pointed to the arrivals-and-departures monitor. "Their plane just landed."

Mel rubbed her hands together. "I hope they're not too mad at me."

Carrie nudged her shoulder. "They're gonna be thrilled to see you."

"That doesn't mean they won't be mad."

Kristy thought back to the night she'd told her parents about her pregnancy. Both of them had cried. They hadn't *acted* mad, but their disappointment had been palpable. Again, Kristy's maternal defenses rose as she yearned to protect her child.

Carrie and Mel stood as people slowly moved through the doors. Kristy spied her parents, who were clad in traditional Brazilian clothes, immediately.

When they saw the family, both parents raced toward them.

"It's so good to see my girls," Dad cried as he cupped each of their cheeks one by one and kissed their foreheads.

Mom squealed as she hugged each of them in turn. "I've missed you so much."

Dad scooped Noah out of Carrie's arms and nestled him against his chest. "My boy."

"Now, let me see him," Mom scolded as she rushed around Dad to rest her chin on his shoulder.

Noah's bottom lip quivered, and he squeaked, his warning that a full-fledged fit would soon ensue. Mom and Dad puckered their lips and cooed and tickled his chin, but another squeak escaped.

Carrie reached for him. "He's getting ready to blow."

Mom swatted Carrie away. "Oh, now, he'll be fine."

As soon as the words left her mouth, a bloodcurdling scream shattered the air. Dad quickly passed the baby back to Carrie. "Maybe he'll need a day or two to adjust to us."

Kristy laughed outright when Carrie pursed her lips and narrowed one eye at their parents.

"And here's our beautiful bride to be." Mom patted Mel's cheeks. "You are glowing, sweetie."

Kristy held her breath as her dad moved closer to Mel. "Now, this boy, he loves the Lord, right?"

"Yes, Grandpa," Mel answered.

Dad looked back at Kristy. "And he's good to my only granddaughter?"

Kristy nodded. "I've been really impressed with their maturity."

Mel stood taller at Kristy's praise. She glanced at each of her grandparents. "You're not mad at me?"

"Oh, honey," her mom cooed. "Your momma was a young mother who didn't have the help of a loving husband, and she was one of the best mothers I've ever known."

Kristy blinked back tears at her mom's compliment.

"That's right," her dad said. "Sometimes people make mistakes, but babies are always blessings."

* * *

Wade opened the church door for Eustace, Ida, Wilma and Dortha. The ladies nodded to him and continued to chatter amongst each other as they walked past him. Eustace stopped and touched his arm. "Kristy doesn't know I'm coming?"

"I haven't been able to get her to talk to me all week, so no, she doesn't."

Eustace worried her bottom lip. "This is all my fault."

"Don't start fretting again. Just do what we talked about. God's got it all worked out already." Despite his confident words, trepidation washed over him. He knew Kristy might not respond to Eustace's admission and apology as they hoped. Wounds sometimes took time to heal.

"Look at this flower arrangement." Ida pointed to the large crystal vase filled with hot-pink-and-purple flowers that sat on the welcome table.

Wilma touched one of the candles displayed around the blooms. "These look like wineglasses."

"I love how they used different sizes to seem like steps going down from the flowers," added Dortha.

"Oh, my." Ida covered her lips with her finger, then pointed at the order of ceremony. "Aren't these adorable?"

"Wonder who came up with the idea?" said Dortha.

Eustace traced her finger along the edge of the photo of Joel and Mel. "I pray God's blessing on their marriage and family."

Wilma wrapped her arm around Eustace's shoulders. "Let's go find Kristy so you can talk with her. You want me to go with you?"

"No. I need to do this myself."

"Do you mind if I go?" asked Wade. Five days had passed since he'd last spoken with Kristy. His heart ached every minute of the separation. He missed her support in his ministry as pastor, her insights, her conversation, her laughter, her kisses. The week had confirmed his desire to make her his wife. The sooner, the better.

Eustace nodded her head one time. "That would be fine. Might even be good."

"She was avoiding me, but I'm pretty sure I saw her slip into the flower room."

Eustace made a beeline for the room, and Wade had to pick up the pace to keep up with her. She opened the door, and Kristy gasped. She was alone. Eustace stepped in, and Wade followed her and shut the door behind them.

Kristy looked back down at the vase in her hand. Wade cringed. If she was trying to make a pretty arrangement, she wasn't doing a very good job. Long stems poked out at wrong angles, and the biggest pink flower was smashed into the top of the container.

"I'd like to enjoy a pleasant day for my daughter. Please."

Eustace walked to Kristy, took the urn from her and set it on a nearby table. Kristy's back stiffened, but she didn't move when Eustace grasped Kristy's hands in hers. "Please forgive a foolish old woman."

Wade swallowed the knot in his throat and shoved his hands deep into his front pockets as Eustace shared everything about her past with the woman he loved. Tears brimmed in Kristy's eyes, and she pulled away from Eustace's grasp and wiped her eyes with her fingertips.

Eustace ended her story with a long exhale. "Please forgive me."

Kristy leaned over and wrapped her arms around Eustace. The older woman welcomed the embrace. "Of course, I do. I understand all you've felt."

Eustace pulled away. "Okay, then. I'm going to go see how I can help." She took the flowers and vase off the table. "I don't think arranging flowers is your gift."

"I know." Kristy sighed. "I keep telling Leah that no one is going to like my crafts."

Eustace jutted her thumb toward Wade. "Our pastor seems to really like you, even if you can't arrange flowers. Why don't you talk to him a minute?" She winked as she opened the door and slipped out of the room.

He leaned against the door. "I'm not letting you out until we talk."

Kristy dipped her chin, then glanced up at him. Her eyelashes splayed across her cheeks, and Wade had to hold back the urge to tip up her face and take her lips as his own.

She smacked her palm against her side. "I'll go to church somewhere else. To make things easier on you."

He grabbed her wrist and then rocked back on his heels. "I'm not sure I can continue to preach here without you by my side." He lifted his brows. "And you know this congregation has really started to like me."

A slow smile spread across her lips. "Are you threatening me, Mr. Humility?"

Mouth tilting up at the corners, he said, "I think I am."

She placed both fists on her hips. "I'm not sure that's the Christian thing to do, *Pastor*."

"Then I guess you better hang out with me a little more." He stepped closer to her and cupped her chin with his palm. He pressed a quick, tender kiss to her lips.

She took a step back. "There will always be someone who will think less of you for being married to a woman who had a child out of wedlock."

"There will also be people who will look down on me for causing my fiancée's death. I was speeding. Breaking the law. I have sinned, as well." He took her hands in his. "We can't live in defeat by our past mistakes."

Kristy chewed her bottom lip for several moments before wrapping her arms around him. "I missed you so much this week."

He kissed the top of her head, then breathed in the luscious fruit scent of her shampoo. "Your parents are here, aren't they?"

"Yes."

"I'd like to meet them."

"They want to meet you, too. Mel and Carrie have been singing your praises fairly consistently this week."

"Then let's go."

They headed toward the church's kitchen, with Wade determined to have a talk with Kristy's father before the wedding. Mother of the bride and soon-to-be grandmother or not, he planned to ask her dad for his blessing on their marriage as soon as he possibly could. If Wade had his way, they'd tie the knot before her parents went back to Brazil.

Chapter 21

Kristy buttoned the back of Mel's wedding dress and then stood beside her daughter and looked at her reflection in the full-length mirror. The straight dress fit Mel perfectly, with just the smallest hint Kristy's grandchild rested in Mel's belly.

"I should have listened to you and gotten a fuller dress," Mel whimpered as she touched her stomach.

"You're breathtaking." Kristy adjusted the fabric around Mel's shoulders. "This dress is perfect on you."

"You're the most beautiful bride ever." Tim's voice sounded behind them.

Mel walked to Tim and gave him a hug. "Thanks, Dad."

Leah peeked through an adjoining room and motioned to Mel. "Come on in here. Let's get your veil on."

"Okay."

Mel walked to the other room, and Kristy followed behind her. Tim touched her arm, and she stopped and turned to him. "You've been really good about letting Leah take part in this."

You mean take over, Kristy thought, but she didn't say the words aloud. "She's been terrific. She knows so much more about all this than I do."

"Yeah, but you could have put up a fight. I mean, she's the stepmom. I know she can be a little overbearing, even if she does really care about Mel."

Kristy raised one eyebrow. "A little?"

Tim grinned.

"Mel cares about her, too," Kristy admitted.

Tim adjusted his bow tie. "She's had a good time planning and spending money." He rolled his eyes and chortled. "Mel's invited us to church a couple times."

"You should come." With the words said, Kristy realized she really was all right if Tim and Leah came to church—her church. They needed the Lord as much as she did. She also realized the jealousy she felt toward Tim and Leah had disappeared. She no longer wanted their lives. Having forgiven herself, she found she wanted her own life. The one God had planned for her. One she hoped might include a good-looking pastor.

"We might do that." Tim popped a mint in his mouth. "I just wanted to say thanks."

Kristy joined Mel and the rest of the girls in the other room. She glanced at Leah, who looked gorgeous in a full-length purple dress. Leah bent down and adjusted a bobby pin in Mel's hair, then motioned for Kristy to stand beside her. "What do you think?"

Mel looked up at her through tulle that stopped just below her chin and then circled around to the base of her neck. Tiny rhinestones dotted the material around her head, and a large silk flower outlined with pearls and rhinestones nestled behind her right ear. Tears filled Kristy's eyes. "Oh, Mel."

"She's lovely, isn't she?" said Leah.

On impulse, Kristy gave Leah a hug. "You have done such a good job making this day special."

Kristy took Mel's hand and lifted it until her daughter stood up. She took her back to the full-length mirror. "Your dad's right. The most beautiful bride ever."

Lights flashed several times beside them. "Those are gonna be great. You're stunning." And Kristy felt stunning in her new dress. The photographer gave them a thumbs-up. "But I've been sent in here to tell you it's time to line up."

"Mom, I'm feeling sick."

"Like puke sick or nervous sick?"

"Nervous."

"Everything's gonna be fine. Joel is a wonderful young man, and you're putting God at the center of your marriage."

Mel fanned her face with a tissue. "Mom, I really think I need to cool down."

Looking around the room, Kristy spied a fan in the corner. She dragged a metal chair over to it, then sat Mel down. Turning on the fan, she held it in front of Mel's face as she took deep breaths in and out. "Getting better?"

Mel's hands shook, but she nodded. "Don't stop for a minute, okay?"

"I won't. Moms are always ready to help their babies when they're sick."

"Or nervous." Mel blew out another breath.

"That's right."

"You're a good mom." Tears brimmed in Mel's eyes, and her chin quivered. "I hope I can be a good mom, too."

"You'll be even better than me." Kristy grabbed a tissue

from the box on the windowsill. She dabbed at Mel's eyes. "Now stop that, or Leah's gonna get both of us."

Mel chuckled. "I think I'm almost ready."

Kristy held Mel's hand as they walked to the back of the church. Before letting go, she squeezed and whispered, "I'm really proud of you."

Taking the usher's elbow, within moments, the doors opened and Kristy walked down the aisle to take a seat on the front row. She locked gazes with Wade. He looked handsome in a black suit and purple silk tie. She loved him so much more than she'd ever thought possible.

She took her seat beside her mom and dad. Dad held a sleeping Noah to his chest. Carrie would walk down the aisle as one of the bridesmaids in a matter of moments. She looked at Joel, who seemed unable to stop fidgeting. He and Mel were so young. She could only pray they allowed God to guide them.

The music started, and one bridesmaid after another walked down the aisle and took their places on the steps of the stage. The ushers closed the doors, and the music changed to the "Bridal Chorus." With the guests, Kristy stood, and the doors opened again.

She glanced at Joel and saw that he'd stopped fidgeting. A full smile wrapped his face, and he wiped his eyes. Looking back at her daughter, she feared her heart would burst with excitement for all God had planned for her. God's plans. Not Kristy's.

Tim and Mel stopped at the end of the aisle long enough for Tim to declare that he and Kristy were giving her away. Joel took Mel's hands in his, and Kristy studied her child's expressions as she pledged her life to Joel. The vow was sealed with a kiss, and Wade proclaimed them husband and wife. The whole thing seemed surreal as the usher came back, took her arm and guided her back up the aisle.

She stood to the side as the photographer captured pictures of Mel and Joel making silly and serious faces with the wedding party and some of the guests. Her heart pounded, and she fought back the urge to burst into tears because her baby had *really* just got married.

"She looks happy," Wade's low voice sounded beside her.

"She does."

The camera flashed as Mel made a duck face while Joel kissed her cheek.

"You're gonna be okay. Eventually."

Kristy grabbed Wade's hand. Though he'd never married or had a child, he seemed to understand her feelings perfectly. With him by her side, she *would* be okay.

Wade watched Kristy as she watched Mel and Joel get into his truck. The groomsmen had written on each of the windows with pink-and-purple window paint. Pink-and-purple balloons and empty water bottles were tied to the bed of the truck. Wade wrapped his arm around Kristy's shoulders when Mel leaned out the window and waved as Joel drove away.

They walked back into the reception area and sat down at the table. Her parents stood together beside the punch bowl. Her mom held Noah up while her dad made faces at him.

"You all right?" Wade asked.

"I'm better than I thought I'd be." She picked a pink flower out of the arrangement at the center of the table and smelled it. "I suppose that's because you're with me."

Wade looked around the room. He'd hoped more of the guests would have left when Mel and Joel had, but many had gone back for more cake or stayed to slow dance at the front of the room. "Wonder when we'll start cleaning up."

Kristy pointed to Leah, who appeared to be in deep, intimate conversation with Tim. "Whenever the boss says, and she doesn't appear to be ready."

"She drove you crazy, huh?"

"Actually, not too bad." She stuck the flower back in the vase, and then took a sip of her drink. "Mel felt a little overwhelmed at times." She placed her cup back on the tablecloth. "Tim said he and Leah might come to church sometime."

Wade nodded. "You're okay with that?"

"I am. I'm not jealous of what they have anymore."

He rubbed sweaty palms against his pants, and then grabbed her hand. "Come on."

She stumbled to her feet. "Wait a minute. I took my heels off."

She started to bend down, and he tugged her hand. "You don't need them."

"Wade," she complained. He continued down the hall and out the side door. "Where are we going?"

The sun had just set over the horizon. Yellow and gold hues still mingled in the distance with pinks and blues, painting a beautiful picture just above them. She stepped on a rock and let out a low grunt. He wished he'd been patient enough to let her put her shoes back on. There was nothing he could do about that now.

Slowing down, he continued to guide her to a small bench overlooking the bass pond. The White Tank Mountains stood majestically in the distance. He sat and tugged her down beside him. Some of her brown waves had fallen out of the clip at the side of her head. He brushed the wayward strands behind her ear.

"Am I starting to look a little scary?" She scrunched her nose and smiled. He devoured each freckle that dotted her cheeks. Her lips taunted him.

"No," he whispered. "Just the opposite."

His heart pounded in his chest. He moved his leg and felt the sharp corner of the box in his pocket. A thousand times, he'd gone over all he wanted to say to her, but looking at her now, he couldn't remember a single thing.

She frowned and touched his jaw with her soft palm. "What's wrong? You look worried."

She had no idea. He feared she'd laugh in his face. They hadn't known each other long. Had barely dated officially. And yet he knew she was the one for him. He didn't want to wait another year or two. He wanted her to be his wife. Soon.

He slid down to one knee and wrapped both her hands in his. Her eyes widened. Words escaped him. His throat felt parched as he tried to remember something he'd planned to say. His fingers shook as he pulled the box from his front pocket. "I love you, Kristy."

She pulled her hands away and covered her mouth. He touched the top of the small container. "I had...all these things... Plans... What I wanted to say. My mind..." His words jumbled together, and he shook his head.

Kristy nodded with tears filling her eyes.

"It's not been long...but I know...in my heart." Exasperated, he opened the box, and Kristy let out a muffled squeal.

"Will you marry me?"

She wrapped her arms around his neck, then sat up and offered her ring finger. "I thought you'd never ask."

Wade slid the square-cut solitaire on her finger and then brushed his lips against hers. "Thought I'd never get past the stuttering, huh?"

She draped her arms over his shoulders. "That, and I knew you asked my dad."

"What? He wasn't supposed to tell you."

"He didn't. I figured it out when the two of you were setting up chairs last night."

"Well, when did you think I'd ask?"

"Then."

"When?"

"Last night."

"I wanted you to enjoy Mel's day first."

She pressed a full kiss against his lips. "Which is only one of the many reasons I love you."

"There was another thing I queried your dad about."

"Queried?"

"Gotta keep you on your toes with the vocabulary."

She laughed. "What's that?"

"I asked if they could extend their stay in the United States an extra week."

"What did they say?"

"He made a few phone calls and found out they could."

"Great."

"You wanna know why I want them to stay?"

"Why?"

"I'd like to get married."

Kristy dropped her arms. "When?"

"As soon as Mel and Joel get back from their honeymoon. What do you think?"

Uncertainty trailed through his body again as she stared at him and blinked for a few moments. Her expression softened, and she molded herself into his arms. "I think that sounds great."

Epilogue

One year later

After the church service ended, Kristy made her way to the nursery. Eustace smiled and waved her inside the room. Kristy traced her finger across her son's soft forehead. "How'd he do for his first time in here?"

Eustace lifted him higher, and Kristy took her son in her arms. "Took his bottle. Got his diaper changed. Then fell asleep."

"He only woke up once last night." Kristy kissed his cheek. "And he might have gone back to sleep on his own if Bo hadn't whined and nudged Wade until he finally went and picked him up."

"No fair." Carrie grabbed for Noah, who cackled and ran away from her. "He's almost fifteen months and still doesn't sleep through the night."

Kristy looked around the room. "Where's my other big guy?"

Eustace pointed to the adjoining room. "Ida's got him in there. She's got a sweet spot for that one."

"I've got him now," said Mel as she scooped up Benjamin's diaper bag off the shelf.

With her free hand, Kristy tickled her grandson's belly. "What are you doing? Were you a good boy for Miss Ida?"

Benjamin kicked his legs and waved his arms up and down. Mel raked her fingers through his unruly curls. "The kid's six months and desperately needs a haircut."

"Don't you dare cut off those beautiful blond curls."

Joel stepped inside the door, and Benjamin squealed and reached for his dad. "Don't you worry, Kristy. I won't let her cut 'em."

Joel hefted Benjamin high in the air, then blew bubbles on his belly. The baby squealed with delight as he grasped at Joel's hair.

Mel lifted her arms and opened her hands. "Can I hold my little brother?"

"May you?"

Mel huffed. "Come on, Mom. I've passed all my English classes. You can't still correct my grammar."

"Actually, I can, meaning I am physically able."

Mel narrowed her gaze as she snatched Micah from Kristy's arms. Micah opened his eyes and puckered his lips. Mel tapped his nose. "How's my little brother doing?"

Carrie reached for Noah, who managed to escape her grasp once again. "Are we still having some girl time today? I need a break."

"You sure are." Wade walked into the nursery and snatched Micah from Mel's arms.

"Hey!" Kristy feigned anger.

"My turn." Wade kissed their baby's head, then pecked Kristy on the lips. "We're having some male bonding time today, aren't we, bud?"

"What kind of male bonding time are you planning?" asked Kristy.

"Thought we'd take Bo for a walk."

"Without me?"

"I think I can handle it." Wade leaned over toward Mel and mumbled, "Your mother is ridiculously protective of your brother."

Joel pointed to Mel. "Now I know where she gets it."

Wade took the burp cloth from Kristy, placed it on his shirt and rearranged Micah so that he rested on Wade's shoulder. "If you don't trust me, then trust Bo. That dog isn't going to let anything happen to his baby."

Kristy grinned when she thought of the last time they'd gone for a walk. Micah had started to fuss, and Bo had plopped down in a sitting position and refused to move. He'd even stuck his nose in the stroller to assist her in getting the pacifier back in Micah's mouth.

"I can't help it that I'm overly protective. It's a maternal thing," Kristy said.

Carrie raced by them until she caught Noah and scooped him up. He shrieked and straightened his back, trying to get her to let him down. "I'm maternal, but I'm all right with Michael watching Noah today."

Michael grimaced. "I can't wait."

Carrie punched his gut, and Michael lifted his hands. "I'm kidding. The kid's a spitfire 'cause he takes after his old dad."

Wade turned around. "Eustace, you were in the nursery today?"

"Sure was."

"The boy was in good hands, then."

She grinned. "He was, at that."

"When are you going back to Maryland?"

She sat up straighter and puffed out her chest. "Labor Day weekend. Can't get here any quicker."

Kristy and Wade had encouraged her to try to find her son. They contacted the hospital and then the adoption agency. Within a month, they'd learned her son had been looking for her for years. She had four grandchildren, two boys and two girls, and six great-grandchildren.

A couple who'd been visiting the church a few weeks walked in to pick up their child. Wade spoke with them a few minutes while Kristy gathered Micah's things.

"Bye, Mom. See you in a little bit," Mel said as she and Joel walked out the door.

Wade followed behind them. Kristy realized she'd left her Bible and Sunday-school material in the adjoining room. She was walking to the other side when she heard the woman's voice. "Was that baby the pastor's son?"

"Sure was," Eustace responded.

"Was that woman with the older baby his daughter?"

"Stepdaughter."

"So the bigger baby is the littler baby's nephew?"

"You've figured it out, and it's the neatest story how that all came to be."

Kristy walked out of the nursery before Eustace began the tale. She thought she'd never recover from the title of being a teenage-pregnancy statistic. Now she'd become a thirtysomething grandma and mom-again statistic. Though she didn't recommend the route she'd taken in the beginning, she wouldn't change the blessings and teaching God had given her along the way.

She walked outside and slipped into the car beside Wade. Peeking in the back, she saw Micah sleeping contentedly in his car seat. Wade rubbed his thumb against the top of her hand. "You seem contemplative."

Kristy smiled. He still hadn't found a word that she didn't know the meaning of. "You're right. I am thinking."

"Good things?"

She thought of how far God had brought her in her walk with Him, in such a short time. She thought of Joel and Mel. They weren't living without trials, but they loved each other and they took good care of Benjamin. And Mel was even in school, as Kristy had wanted. She thought of Wade and Micah and how never in her wildest dreams would she have thought God would bless her with them. She turned to Wade. "Very good things."

He shuffled his brows and offered a mischievous smile. "Do the good things have to do with me?"

Kristy leaned toward him and cupped his jaw with both hands. "Let me answer that for you." Then she claimed his lips with hers. She'd never tire of his kiss.

* * * * *

REQUEST YOUR FREE BOOKS!

2 FREE INSPIRATIONAL NOVELS
PLUS 2
FREE
MYSTERY GIFTS

Love Inspired

REQUEST YOUR FREE BOOKS!

2 FREE INSPIRATIONAL NOVELS
PLUS 2
FREE
MYSTERY GIFTS

Love Inspired
HISTORICAL
INSPIRATIONAL HISTORICAL ROMANCE

ReaderService.com

Manage your account online!

- Review your order history
- Manage your payments
- Update your address

***We've designed
the Harlequin® Reader Service
website just for you.***

Enjoy all the features!

- Reader excerpts from any series
- Respond to mailings and
  special monthly offers
- Discover new series available to you
- Browse the Bonus Bucks catalog
- Share your feedback

Visit us at:
ReaderService.com